I0646420

From reviews of *Choosing Life in Israel* (a selection of articles by P. David Hornik published in 2013):

"Hornik has become one of Israel's best-informed and most astute journalists."

—Edward Alexander, *Chicago Jewish Star*

"Hornik's book is a compendium of personal and political essays he has written since he became one of Israel's most incisive journalists. Arranged in chronological order, they revisit in eloquent prose a besieged nation's triumphs and tragedies, its ancient stones and its modern cities, its beauty, its warts…and its holiness."

—Ruth King, *Family Security Matters*

From a customer review for *You Beside the Still Waters* (a novel by P. David Hornik published by Adelaide Books in 2019), appearing both on the Amazon page and at goodreads.com:

"a wonderfully written and richly descriptive novel with brilliantly drawn characters…. The author weaves a well-crafted contemporary romance…a fascinating and captivating read that had me immersed from the beginning."

—Piaras O Cionnaoith

AND BOTH SHALL ROW

And Both Shall Row

a novel
by

P. DAVID HORNIK

Adelaide Books
New York / Lisbon
2020

AND BOTH SHALL ROW
a novel
by P. David Hornik

Copyright © by P. David Hornik
Cover design © 2020 Adelaide Books

Published by Adelaide Books, New York / Lisbon
adelaidebooks.org

Editor-in-Chief
Stevan V. Nikolic

All rights reserved. No part of this book may be reproduced in any manner whatsoever without written permission from the author except in the case of brief quotations embodied in critical articles and reviews.

For any information, please address Adelaide Books
at info@adelaidebooks.org
or write to:
Adelaide Books
244 Fifth Ave. Suite D27
New York, NY, 10001

ISBN: 978-1-952570-96-4

Printed in the United States of America

Contents

PART ONE: AUGUST 1970

1

As he lay in his room, half-awake, he became aware of voices. They were coming from the adjoining bungalow, the one on the left. People there. A few people. A family, most likely. Maybe, at last, something…

It was mid-morning, already hot in the room. They were at the vacation bungalow on Blue Spruce Lake. When he was a kid, he loved coming here; now, he was bored. In the bungalow on the right, there was an old couple. In the bungalow on the left, there had been—up to now—no one. And nothing to see, either, at the little beach that served the row of about a dozen bungalows—Pleasant Cove, they were called—that faced the lake. If you had to be at a place like this for two weeks, you could hope there would at least be some girls to look at, maybe even meet. But so far there'd been none.

It wasn't the only reason he was bored. When he was a kid, it was a thrill, a joy, just to swim out in the lake, to climb onto the raft and jump from it, to go for rowboat rides with dad (not that dad was available for that very often). And, of course, to read; by the time he was six, seven, it was already a passion. Zane Grey, Edgar Rice Burroughs, Jack London, Alistair MacLean, James Fenimore Cooper, Howard Fast, Max Brand, Daniel Defoe, Kenneth Roberts, and so many others.

And to read these wonderful books up here, in the mountain air with the pine smell, was even more enjoyable.

But now he didn't read so much. When he tried to read a book, it had to really talk to him, really hit the spot, and there weren't many that did that. What did these books know about him and his friends, about their lives in—and outside of—Willowcreek High? Really nothing. As for swimming in the lake, jumping from the raft—it wasn't, of course, what it used to be. Which didn't leave much to do, up here, in the "vacation." He didn't like the bungalow's close quarters, either. Him in one bedroom, his sister in another, his parents in another, all three rooms so crammed together you felt everyone was spying on everyone else.

But now...noise from the other bungalow. A screen door slapping shut, voices—a girl's voice? It seemed that way but probably he'd imagined it.

His sister was at the kitchen table, studiously eating corn flakes. His mother was washing dishes. Nine-thirty; the window showed the whitish sky of another hot August day in the Adirondack Mountains.

"You look," his sister said, "like you've got to go back to bed and try getting up again."

Lizzie was thirteen, three years younger than him. She had frizzy carrot-colored hair, frank blue eyes, pink cheeks, pale skin. In the last couple of years she'd gotten pudgy. When he was younger they'd been great friends; now not so much.

He pulled out a chair, loudly scraping its legs on the floor, and slumped into it. He sat there, rubbing his eyes.

"Kenny!" his mother said. "Sorry, but you're a little late for the pancake hour."

"Oh, that's OK mom. Could I just have coffee?"

"That's all you want?"

"Yeah. Maybe, a cookie or something, I don't know..."

His mother was on the tall side and broad-shouldered, with straight silky-blond hair. She was principal of an elite girls' school in Schenectady, a town near where they lived. She earned—this he was now old enough to understand—most of their money. His father—now out on the porch with his type-writer—was a writer but didn't earn that much money from it.

"You look," said Lizzie, "like you haven't recovered from a sleeping-pill overdose."

"You look," he said, "like something that was rescued from the disaster area."

"Kids," his mother said.

When he walked out on the front porch, wearing a T-shirt, swim-ming trunks, and thongs, a towel slung over his shoulder, his fa-ther was—of course—sitting there to his left. At the large round table in the shade at that corner of the porch. On the table was a typewriter with a piece of paper in the carriage, on its right side a neat stack of blank pieces of paper, on its left side a strewn mess of pieces of paper with various amounts of typing on them.

"Kenny!" his father said, looking up at him—eagerly, as if seizing a deliverance from something.

"Hi, dad."

"Going for a swim! Well. You haven't done that in a while. I mean, so early."

"Yeah. Guess I felt like it."

His father was on the short side, with dark curls in a fan-like shape around his head, bright, dark eyes. He wrote novels, and though he wrote them steadily and the small publisher he had kept publishing them, he wasn't famous. Kenny had years ago given up mentioning his name—Nathan Wasserman—in the hope that people had heard of him. The novels—he'd never read one of them, but he'd glanced through them when he was home alone—were always short and seemed to be dramas about ordinary people with ordinary problems, usually involving failed love affairs.

"*This*...," his father said. He sat back, ran tense fingers through his curls, gazed in something like stupefaction at the page he was typing. "You wouldn't believe it...."

"Making trouble for you?"

"*Oh*..." He gazed brightly at Kenny. "You take it in one direction, it wants to go in twenty-nine other directions."

"Well, maybe you should take a break."

"A break." He gazed at the page and up at Kenny again, as if there were something hopelessly perplexing in this thought. "I probably should. I probably should."

"Well."

"Have a nice swim!"

"OK."

His eyes keenly scouted the beach as he drew up to it. But there were just a few of the same people who'd been there since they'd started this "vacation" a few days ago. There was one woman, a wife and mother, maybe twenty-five, who looked pretty good in her one-piece swimsuit. But it wasn't something you'd come down to the beach just to see.

The sky looked hot and heavy; the locusts trilled like a tiny high-pitched chainsaw; the lake—a quite large lake well into the mountains, north of Lake George—looked drowsy, already listless in the heat. He tossed his towel on the sand, took off his shirt and dropped it beside the towel, kicked off his thongs, and walked up to the water. Might as well swim. What difference did it make?

2

Outside his window at the bungalow there were a couple of birch trees, and he liked how they looked at the dusk hour. The same white, but somehow appearing more delicate in the grey-blue dusk color.

But staring out the window now, in the latter dusk, the day slowly dying, the birches were—still—the only thing to see. The other bungalow was quiet. It looked empty and deserted as it had looked in the days before this morning.

He lay back down on his bed, fingers twined behind his head, looking at the ceiling.

He could hear the noises in his own bungalow. Soon they'd be asking him to join them in the Scrabble game. Up here in the bungalow, they played every evening. Yes, it was fun—he could admit that. He, his father, and his mother were all pretty good players, though his father was the best and usually won. Lizzie got frustrated because she didn't win, but she was better now and this summer had won once and been hugely thrilled about it.

Yes, he'd heard noises from the other bungalow now and then during the day; there was definitely someone there. In the afternoon, following soon after his mother and Lizzie—his father was still on the porch—he'd gone down to the beach again. And again, nothing. Well, not exactly nothing; there were people who hadn't been there before, a man and a kid, the kid maybe Lizzie's age. But he knew that there were other people, too, in the other bungalow—he'd heard voices, female voices. A girl's voice. But maybe he'd imagined it. Probably he'd imagined it....

As he made his way to the front door, they'd already sat down for the Scrabble game at the dining table—the table at one end of the living room, nearest the kitchen, where they ate lunch and supper, and played Scrabble in the evening.

"Kenny!" his father said. "Where you going!"

"Just out for a walk."

"Come back soon! We want to get going with our game here!"

"No, that's OK."

He turned to face them. His father was setting out the board and the letter racks as his mother and Lizzie looked on.

He said—standing with his hand on the knob of the door—"I'm going to take a walk, uh, for a while. You should just get started."

"Feeling OK?" his mother said.

"Yeah. Fine. I just…I don't know, kind of restless. Feel like walking a little."

A full, or nearly full, moon had risen across the lake. Its light lay like a vague, silvery mist over the dark water.

He went slowly, picking his way down the plank steps that led down to the beach. He'd had to get out of there; he couldn't lie around anymore and he couldn't be with them anymore. Out here there was just the mountain night, the forms of pines around him.

He came to the beach, walked out on it, and stopped.

He heard the lapping of ripples.

From here the moonlight appeared as a long flame across the water.

He stood and felt the night, the silence.

As he stood there he realized that—not far from him, to the right, closer to the water than he was—someone was sitting in one of the beach chairs.

He peered.

It was a girl—with very long, dark hair.

He said, "Hey."

"Hey."

The voice conveyed no surprise; she'd known he was there.

He walked forward; stopped, almost beside the chair, a little behind it.

He said, "You from 8?"

Her left arm on the armrest, she turned and peered at him. "What?"

"You from 8?"

She looked at him a moment longer, then turned back toward the lake.

"8, what's that. I don't know what you're talking about."

"Bungalow 8. I'm in Bungalow 7. I think you're in the one next to mine."

She sunk her face into her hands, sighed.

"I don't think I really know what number it is."

He inched closer, so that he was standing parallel to her.

She said—still with her face in her hands—"You always stand up when you talk to people?"

He gazed toward her.

"No. Not always. Maybe some of the time. I'll get a chair."

They were thrown together on the left side of the beach near the dock where the two rowboats were tethered. They were white metal chairs, and he didn't like them; you had to sink way down in them, feel that your arms on the armrests were always pulling you up.

He dragged one of them across the sand and set it next to hers. He plopped down in it.

The moon looked incredibly bright over the inkily black hills.

Her elbows were on the armrests and her chin in her hands; she seemed to be staring gravely at the lake, in an absorption that did not include him.

He said, "So...you came here today?"

She sighed; she turned and looked at him as if surprised, as if she'd forgotten he was there.

"Today. Yeah. This morning."

He said, "I think I might have seen your father and brother down here before. If that's who they were."

She said, "That's not my father."

"So what is he?"

"What is he? I'd like to know that. I'd really like to know what he is."

She said, "He's just somebody my mother married."

She said—looking at him more intently now—"What's your name?"

He looked at her. He could make out an oval face framed by very bountiful black hair.

"My name's Kenny. What's yours?"

"Colleen."

"Where you from?"

"You haven't heard of it."

"So tell me anyway."

"Pasamanack."

"Pasamanack. No, can't say I've heard of that."

He said, "Where is it?"

"You haven't heard of that either."

"Where you from, the moon?"

"New Jersey."

"New Jersey. I've heard of that."

He said, "What are you doing all the way up here?"

She sighed long and deep, as if it were painful to have to deal with this question.

"Ever look at a map of New Jersey?"

"A map of New Jersey. I don't think so. I may have sometime. I don't think so."

"Well, if you did you'd see that it's not full of big tourist places."

"Tourist places… Atlantic City's there, isn't it?"

"Yeah. But it's a little different from this place."

"Yeah. It is. If you want something quiet."

"Right. Quiet."

She said, "That's what I can't stand."

She said, "I hate having to be here."

"Yeah?" he said.

She said, "Too quiet."

She said, "I begged my mother and the jerk not to have to come here. Of course they didn't trust me to be alone in the house for a week. They were sure I'd open a massage parlor."

"You're only here for a week?"

"Yeah. Thank God."

She said, "At home…I don't know. My friends kind of distract me. Up here…" she raised her hands and dropped them on the armrests. "Nothing to do. End up just thinking. Just…thinking."

She turned toward him; seemed to ponder him.

She said, "You seem like you might be better than nothing."

He burrowed back into the chair.

"Colleen, thanks. That's really…a great compliment."

She kept gazing at him.

She said, "Do you have a girlfriend?"

"Do I have a girlfriend. No. Not at the moment."

"Why not?"

"Why not? I don't know."

"You look like someone who would have one."

"Look like someone who would have one. Why. Why do I look like that?"

"I don't know. You look like someone girls would go after."

He flicked his fingers through his hair. "Well, thanks."

"You're pretty shy."

"Shy?"

"Here you're sitting with me in the dark. No one else here. And you don't make a move or anything."

He looked at the moon—as if seeking help from it.

He said, "You don't seem like you're in a good mood."

"So what. What guy cares about that?"

She said, "What guy cares about how the girl feels."

"Colleen, some guys do care about it."

She sat forward again; sunk her head in her hands again.

He looked at the moon, entranced by how it sat and shone.

She said, "My brother got killed in Vietnam."

He looked at her very slowly. She was sitting hunched up in herself.

"What?"

He said, "When was it?"

"Two years ago. The Tet Offensive."

She said, "Some Viet Cong laid an ambush for his squad. He was the lieutenant, he was leading them, and he was the one that got killed. Blown away by a machinegun. Blown to bits."

"Oh my God."

He said, "Colleen, that's…I'm really sorry."

She removed her hands from her face; sat back again and stared forward.

He said, "Oh boy… I can't imagine what something like that's like."

She sat as if she hadn't heard him.

She turned and pondered him again.

She said, "So where are you from?"

"Oh, you haven't heard of that either."

"OK, so, what? What is it?"

"It's about two hours south of here. It's called Willowcreek Park. Not too far from Albany. Closer to Schenectady, but you probably haven't heard of that either."

"Albany's the capital of this state, right?"

"Right."

"Why did they make Albany the capital instead of New York City?"

"I don't know. It's a good question. I've never understood it."

"So what do you do in Menlo Park or whatever it is?"

"Willowcreek Park."

"Willowcreek Park."

"What do I do?"

He folded his arms, stared forward, thought.

"I don't know. I live, I guess. I hang around with my friends. We play basketball. We drink beer."

"You don't seem like a jock."

He grinned. "No, I wouldn't say that's what I am."

He said, "I'm kind of good at basketball. I was on JV this year. I wouldn't say I'm the classic jock though."

"So you're going into eleventh?"

"Yup."

"Well, so am I."

She said, "So there are no girls in this?"

"What?"

"No girls involved in what you do? Playing basketball, drinking beer?"

"No. No, I didn't say that."

He said, "I had a girlfriend this year. It was a couple of months."

"What was her name?"

"Celeste."

"Celeste? That's a pretty name."

"Yeah, I guess you could say that."

He stretched his arms, moving them in circles, trying to relieve the discomfort from their resting on the armrests.

She said, "Why did you come down here tonight?"

"Why did I come down here?"

"Yeah, because if you look around, you see that there aren't a lot of people coming down here at night. So there would have to be some kind of reason for it."

"Just restless, I guess. Felt cooped up. I don't know, it's hard being cooped up with the same people for two weeks."

He said, "I'm kind an introvert, I guess. I can't stand the feeling that everyone sees what I'm doing."

"An introvert."

"Yeah."

"You said you have friends."

"Well. Introverts can have friends."

He said, "I have one really close friend, a couple of good pals, and loads of 'Hey, how you doin'' people."

"So who is this close friend?"

"Uh, his name's Leon."

"Leon?"

"Yeah."

"So who's this Leon?"

"Well...he's quite a guy. We've been friends since fifth grade when his family moved to Willowcreek. He's, like, a real good student, especially in science. Top athlete—he was on JV football, basketball, and baseball this year, and he'll be on varsity next year, on all of them. But. He's kind of wild."

"Wild?"

"Yeah, he just loves to drink and have fun. He's the most fun-loving person I've ever known. Introduced me to beer when I was thirteen."

"Sounds like he's kind of a match for you."

"What do you mean by that?"

"Well, you're kind of quiet, he's fun-loving, so it sounds like he brings out this other side of you."

"Yeah, there's something to that."

"He do drugs too?"

"No. Not yet anyway."

"What, they don't do drugs in your school?"

"Course they do drugs in my school. They do them everywhere now."

He said, "I guess the athletes are more into booze. Couple of the top athletes do drugs now, though."

She said, "My best friend's trying to get me to smoke grass."

"Yeah?"

"Yeah. But she tries to get me to do all kinds of things."

"Like what?"

"Oh, I don't know."

She sighed very deeply, put her face in her hands again.

She said, "I guess you could call me an introvert too. I don't think I used to be one, though. Until all kinds of shit started happening to me."

"What shit?"

She said, "I'll tell you about it sometime."

He sat still.

He said, "So I guess we'll be seeing more of each other."

"Yeah. We're stuck with each other."

"Yeah. And I'm better than nothing."

She gave a very small laugh, letting her face come out of her hands again.

"Don't mind me. I'm kind of a dark, awful person."

"Yeah?"

"Yeah."

He peered at his watch.

He said, "I can't see what time it is, but they're probably wondering where the hell I am. Probably finishing up their game already. Probably shouldn't stay here too much longer."

"It's not really late, is it?"

"No, I don't think so. But they're probably worried. This is the first time I've ever done this, skipped the Scrabble game and gone off for a walk instead. They go to sleep early."

"Early? Why?"

"It has to do with my father. He's really disciplined."

"Disciplined. What is he, a district superintendent?"

"Ha, ha. No, he's a writer. His sleep's real important to him, so he can get up early and get to work for another ten hours."

"A writer."

"Yup."

"What's his name?"

He sighed. "You haven't heard of him. You know, like…the town you live in, and the town I live in. There are things that people just…haven't heard of."

"What's the point of being a writer if no one's heard of him?"

"Colleen, it's a good question. It's just what he loves to do. He's addicted to it. Every year, you know, my mother…she says, please, dear, take it easy this time, at least while we're up at the lake, take a little vacation. And every year it's the same—he just sets up shop on the porch and works the whole time, just like he does at home."

"What's his name?"

"Nathan Wasserman."

"Nope, haven't heard of him."

She said, "There's a kid in my school named Neil Wasserman. He's Jewish."

"Yes. Wasserman is a Jewish name."

She looked at him.

"So now I know two Jewish people in my life, and they're both named Wasserman."

"Nope. You only know one. I'm not Jewish."

She stared at him.

"So you've got a stepfather too?"

"No, he's my real father. You're only supposed to be Jewish if your mother's Jewish. My mother's not."

"Yeah?"

She sat back, looked out at the lake.

"That's weird."

"Well, it's the rule."

"I didn't know that."

He said, "I should be going back up."

"Gotta put daddy to bed?"

"Ha, ha."

She said, "Guess I'll walk up with you."

"You don't have to if you'd rather be here."

"Nah. Probably less boring than just keeping sitting here."

He said, "Would you want to go into Gifford's Landing to-morrow and hang around?"

They were going up the plank steps. The air of the mountain night was cool and fragrant. The pines stood still and somber.

She said, "Into Gifford's Landing… I don't know, it's kind of far to walk."

"We can probably get a ride."

"Yeah, but…I don't know. It's kind of touristy, you know, kind of touristy and noisy. I don't know…I'm sorry I'm like this, I just—I just can't stand crowds, it's the last thing I want right now."

"Oh, that's all right."

He said, "So why don't we meet down at the beach?"

She said, "I can't go down to the beach during the day."

"Oh? Why's that?"

"Because the jerk gawks at me."

"Oh."

He stared down gravely as they plodded up the plank steps.

"OK, here's an idea. What do you say we take one of the rowboats out. You can just wear regular clothes, so he won't gawk at you too much when you come down."

They came to the top of the steps. They turned and faced each other.

She said, "We could do that."

He said, "What time's good for you?"

"I guess afternoon. I try to sleep in the morning. If I sleep at all it's in the morning. I don't sleep much at night."

"Oh… So, two o'clock, that be OK?"

"Let's make it three. When the sun's a little less bright."

"OK… Meet down there, by the dock?"

"Sure."

He reached out and held her wrist.

She said, "I'll see you tomorrow, Kenny."

"OK."

He gingerly let go of her wrist and removed his hand.

She said, "Goodnight."

"Goodnight."

She sent him a small smile as she was turning away from him.

In the bungalow, the only one still left at the dining table was his mother. She was reading the *New York Times* his father had gone into Gifford's Landing to buy very early in the morning.

"Well," his mother said as he came in, still gazing at a page.

He went into the kitchen; he opened some things, put together a sandwich with American cheese and butter.

As he came and stood by the table, his mother looked up brightly at him.

"Well. We wondered where you were."

"Oh, I was just down at the beach."

"Nice out?"

"Yeah."

He said, "Actually, I met someone."

"*Met* someone. At night?"

"Yeah, this girl was down there. This girl who moved into 8."

With her silky-blond hair in bangs on her forehead, her lively hazel eyes, his mother had a youthful, intense look. Only recently had it been occurring to Kenny that this was probably pleasing to his father, giving more balance to a marriage in which she seemed in some ways the dominant figure.

"Oh, I saw that girl. She's very pretty."

"Yeah. They're from…New Jersey."

He stood munching the sandwich.

He said, "Mom, if you try to kiss a girl, and she doesn't let you, does it mean she doesn't like you?"

She gazed brightly at him.

"Not necessarily."

She said, "It might just mean she wants to get to know you better."

"We're supposed to go out in a rowboat tomorrow."

"Oh. Well, she probably wouldn't agree to that if she was totally against you."

"Yeah."

"You might just need to give it time."

"Yup."

He swallowed down—he'd been quite hungry—the last of the sandwich.

"Well," he said. "Night."

"Night," she smiled brightly.

3

At about seven in the morning, he heard it—a man's sudden, sharp cry, as if in amazement or horror. It was from Bungalow 8. It was gone as suddenly as it had been there, leaving the same morning stillness in its wake.

Too groggy to think about it, he turned on his other side and went back to sleep.

He recalled it again when he was going down the plank steps to the beach. It was about ten o'clock. Knowing about the event later in the day with Colleen, he'd felt even more restless; he thought he could at least swim some of it away.

The locusts made the same high, deadly-sounding zing, but the day was brighter and clearer than yesterday. The lake and far hills looked stunningly beautiful. He thought about the sound, the sudden one, earlier in the morning; and realized—one side of his mouth curling up a bit derisively—what it must have been.

Down at the beach he saw the man and the boy again. The man was very tall and thin, the narrow face birdlike, topped with a straight thatch of blond curls; his eyes, meeting

Kenny's once, expressed a dull curiosity, as if searching uncertainly for something. The boy was much smaller, with black hair and darkly tanned, glancing around with black, startled eyes. Kenny noticed that the man and the boy seemed to get along; they played paddleball together for a while before the boy went swimming and the man seated himself on a blanket with a newspaper.

He, himself, intended to swim to the raft, but instead swam far beyond it—farther than you were supposed to. He didn't care; it felt wonderful, at last, to pour all the energy out. He turned over on his back to float; well out in the lake, he gazed straight into the shining blue sky.

This afternoon I'll be in a rowboat with a girl.... He thought about what it would be like—after the vacation, when they were back in Willowcreek Park—to tell Leon about it. Yeah, at first I thought, you know, two weeks of unbelievable boredom—and then you wouldn't believe what turns up there....

When he went back down to the lake toward three o'clock, it was a bright, hot August afternoon and the beach was full of people. His mother and Lizzie were there; and the man and the boy and a woman who must have been Colleen's mother; only his father was still on the porch. And also Colleen—he registered, his eyes quickly scanning the place—wasn't there. Fear gripped him; what if she stood him up? What if she was just playing with him?

Ambling through the sand to the dock, wearing a T-shirt, shorts, and thongs, he saw that one of the two rowboats was there, tethered to the dock. It hadn't occurred to him that *both* of them could have been gone, and then their outing would have been under a question mark. But one of the boats was there; only Colleen wasn't.

He glanced at his watch. It was still a couple of minutes before three.

He shuffled around in the sand. He glanced up periodically at the steps—but not too often, not wanting to appear anxious.

Finally, at ten after three, he spied her coming down the steps.

She looked like the person he'd been with last night; but, at the same time, she didn't look like her. The hair was the same—abundant and flowing, just glossier in the light. But her face wasn't what he would have expected; it had something serene, almost contented about it, and when her blue eyes met his there was something like gentle affection in them, as if he were an old friend she was fond of.

She wore sandals, denim shorts, and a polo shirt with thick horizontal black and white stripes. It was open at the throat, and tight; it seemed to belie her words about not wanting to be looked at too much.

She said, "Hi."

"Hi."

"I'm really sorry, I was like, reading, and I look up and I say, oh my God, it's almost three, and I start dashing around. I'm really sorry I kept you waiting."

"Oh, it's OK. It's only"—he glanced at his watch—"ten after three."

He said, gesturing, "Least we've got a boat."

"A boat?"

"Yeah. There are two rowboats. Somebody took one of them out. If they'd taken both of them out…we're out of luck."

"Oh."

She said, "Guess we'd have had to take a plane."

"A *plane*. I'm not much of a pilot."

"No?"

"Nope."

She was looking in curiosity at the boat; she walked toward it, and he followed her down the dock.

She said, "I've never really gone in one of these things. Maybe once, when I was a little kid."

"No? Well, it ain't hard. You can sit there, facing the rower."

"Yeah? That's all I have to do?"

"That's all you have to do. You get to go forward, too. The rower has to go backwards."

She looked at him with the soft, affectionate look.

"That's really unfair."

"It is. Lot of things are, what can I say."

She reached one hand into the water as the boat, with him rowing, moved out into the lake, out past the beach and swimming area where the people already looked small.

She said, "This is nice."

"Yeah, it is."

She slowly pulled her hand out of the water, watching the trail of drops it made.

She said, "Where we going?"

"Where we *going*? I don't know. Thought we'd just…drift around awhile."

"Don't we have some kind of destination?"

"Destin*ation*."

"Yeah, it seems like…if we're going for a ride, we should have some kind of destination."

"Well," he said, "there's that island down to the south."

He looked over his shoulder and gestured toward it.

She rose a little from her seat, shielding her eyes with her hand. He looked at her body; looked away.

She said, settling back on her seat, "Looks nice."

She said, "Ever been there?"

"Been there? Not really. Passed it a few times with my father."

"It's like…far out in the lake."

"Yeah, the lake's really wide down there."

"What if I tell you I don't know how to swim?"

"Well, I'll tell you there are a couple of lifejackets if it gets to that"—he gestured behind him—"and I wouldn't worry about it anyway."

She glanced behind him at the two orange lifejackets on the floor of the boat.

She said, "If all else fails, will you save me?"

He looked at her.

"Sure."

"Really? You'd dive in and save me?"

"Nah, I'd let you drown. Come on Colleen, what do you think?"

"I don't know."

"You don't know? You don't know what you think?"

"Nope. A lot of the time, I *really* don't know what I think."

"Well, you shouldn't worry about it anyway. The seas shouldn't get too rough at this time of year."

"No?"

"Nope."

"So let's go there."

He shrugged. "OK."

Still not too far from the western, much more populated shore, he let the left-hand oar rest on the water and tugged hard with the right-hand oar, turning the boat southeast.

It turned, and he went back to regular, rhythmic rowing.

She trailed her hand in the water again, lifted it up, watched the drops.

On the left, patches of pine woods alternated with hotel and motel beaches; all very small-looking now, the people more or less a blur.

Points of light danced on the ripples of the lake.

She said, "So, did you hear the jerk this morning?"

He moved his eyes slowly to hers.

He grinned. "Uh, actually, yeah."

"Really? Did it wake you up?"

"Yeah. Just for a minute."

"Can't believe it. Now he's waking the neighbors up too."

"He's getting more airplay."

"He like...does it at weird hours. You know, sometimes it's like, three in the morning, and—*ahhhhh!*"

"Colleen, I'm sorry I'm laughing, I'm sure it's not funny to you."

"Oh, I don't care anymore."

She said, "At home, at least, their bedroom's downstairs. I'm upstairs, so *sometimes* I might not hear it. But up here, you know..."

"Up here everything's damn close together."

"And my mother, like, she's making all kinds of noises too, 'Oh darling,' you know, and all this kind of junk."

"Oh, boy."

He said, "How long have they been married?"

"Couple of years. They were married already when my brother got killed."

"Oh, boy… I guess…I guess that didn't help matters."

"No, having a jerk like that come into your life at a time like that doesn't help matters. Guy who needs it, you know, twice a day at least, nothing's enough for him, *ahhhhh!*"

"Colleen, I'm sorry, I don't mean to laugh."

She reached her hand into the water, tossed drops at him. "I'm sorry."

"Yeah, you should be."

He started turning the boat more toward the right, toward the open lake, where the island was. The shore was quite far now, even the hotel and motel buildings looking small.

She said, "I could try rowing, and give you a break."

"Nah, it's fine."

"It's really nice of you to give me a ride, because…this is really, really peaceful out here."

"Well, glad you like it."

"Could you…give me one of those lifejackets?"

He looked at her. "Why?"

"You'll see."

"Colleen. You can't take a swim out here."

"I'm not taking a swim."

"You're not?"

"No."

"So why do you want a lifejacket?"

"Give it to me and you'll see."

He reached behind him, dug one of them off the floor, hauled it over to her.

She propped it against the ledge of the stern. She leaned way back, nestled her head in it, draped her arms over the sides of the boat.

She said, "Ohhh, this is nice."

The shirt went up on her stomach; he looked at her. He looked at her eyes; they were closed. He looked back at her body. He stopped.

"Kenny," she said, her eyes closed, "this is the first time I've really felt…kind of OK…since they took me to this place."

"Well, I'm glad you're feeling OK."

"You see how smart I was to say we should leave at three? Now the sun's, like, slanted. Just soft…just nice…"

He glanced up at the sun, which was over the hills to the left, to the west. "You're a smart one, Colleen."

She said, "How deep's the water here?"

"Here? I don't know. Deepest point of the lake is a few hundred feet, I think."

"A few hundred feet. Wowww…"

She said, "What do you think it would be like if we just kind of, you know, sank into it, and disappeared?"

"Colleen, I don't think it would be too great."

"*No?* Why not?"

He looked at her. Her eyes were closed, but she was smiling.

"Well, I think some people would be kind of sad."

"Think so? I'm not so sure. About you, yeah, I'm sure. About me…I don't know."

She said, "Kenny, you don't know how many times I've wanted to do that."

"Sink into a lake?"

She laughed.

"No. Not that method exactly."

"You mean…sink. Disappear."

"Yeah."

"Colleen, I'm sorry to hear that."

He said, "I really…I really hope you won't do that."

"You don't have to worry, Kenny."

"No?"

"Nope. Because…I wouldn't do it to Billy."

"Billy. Who's that, your brother?"

"Yeah. It's like…first his big brother's gone. Then his big sister's gone. That's kind of over the top."

"Yeah, I'd say it is."

He said, "I saw him this morning with your stepfather."

He said, "They seemed like they were pretty good friends. I was kind of surprised after what you told me about him. About your stepfather."

"You mean about being a jerk?"

"Yeah."

She sighed deeply; stretched her arms upward with clenched fists, dropped them over the sides of the boat again. This time her shirt rode up further; he looked at her belly, saw it rise and fall as she breathed. He looked away.

"Kenny, you know, it's kind of a thrill for Billy just having some kind of daddy around, because he can't even remember when we had a supposed real daddy living in the house. The other thing is, Billy's a boy, so I don't think he has to worry about the jerk gawking at him and things."

"So he gawks at you?"

"Oh, God… Like in the house, I have to go around like a nun…. At the beach…forget it."

"This is even though he's got an active sex life?"

"Insatiable, Kenny."

"Is your mother aware of this?"

"Is she aware of it? Kenny, I think she would have to be, somewhere deep down. But what's she going to do. I think she's just happy to have nabbed any old jerk."

"Does he bother you?"

Now her eyes opened, slightly; she peered toward him from half-closed lids.

"Bother me...? What do you mean? You mean does he touch me?"

"Yeah."

She closed her eyes again, nestled her head into the life-jacket.

"No...that was the other one's specialty."

"What other one?"

"Kenny...here I'm feeling peaceful, and you're asking tough questions."

"Sorry."

He rowed quietly. The oars plunged into the water; emerged stained, sunlit, and dripping; plunged in again.

"Are we at our island yet?"

He glanced over his shoulder.

"Getting closer. Should be a few more minutes."

4

It was a solitary and small island, dense with pines, broken sunlight lying in patches in glades. Approaching it, he saw a shore that was mainly a wall of jagged rock; but by drifting a little to the south he came to a patch of ground that was part sand, part clumps of rough grass of some sort.

He rowed until the boat edged up on the sand. Colleen was sitting now, watching him guide the boat.

He got out of it, went to the prow. She climbed out of the boat; he tugged it well up on the sand, not taking a chance that it would be anywhere near the water.

He stood up straight and looked at her.

"Well," he said. "What do you think?"

"What do I think?"

"Yeah."

"Well." She stood with her hands on her hips, looking around her. "Well, I think this is a place where I'd probably like to be for good and never have to be anyplace else."

"I'm not sure we'd find that much to eat."

"Must be some kind of berries growing someplace."

"Maybe. Probably not that tasty though."

He said, "Should have brought a blanket or something."

She spread her hands and dropped them to her thighs.

"Kind of thing you don't think of while you can still think of it."

He looked around.

"That tree over there's got a pretty wide trunk."

"What…that one?"

"Yeah… We could try sitting against it."

Their eyes met.

She said, "Well. Can't really expect lounge chairs in a place like this."

"Nah."

He found himself sitting beside her, their backs to the tree trunk, their upper arms pressed together. He pressed his bare right leg into her bare left leg; she moved her leg away.

They were facing toward the western shore, the one they'd come from; it looked very distant and small now.

She said, "Oh, this is too nice."

She said, "Let's take a tent here and just live here."

"You don't think it'd get boring?"

"No I really don't."

"Get kind of cold in the winter."

"We'll bring winter clothes."

"OK. That should do it."

She leaned back against the tree trunk, eyes closed.

The water lapped onto the sand. It sounded more pensive than it did at the other place, the beach.

She said, "Kenny, before…you didn't have to do that."

"Do what."

"When you pushed your leg into mine."

He sat very still.

"Well, I know I didn't have to."

She remained with her head against the trunk, eyes closed.

She said, "I'm sorry I lay back like that in the boat. It was just so nice and peaceful that way."

"It's all right."

"It probably got you stirred up. I'm sorry."

"Colleen it's OK. Really."

"Is it all right if...if it's just like this?"

"Yes, it's fine."

She said, "It would be nice if you'd put your arm around me."

"Well, yeah it would.... I just want to be sure it's all right."

"Yes. It's all right."

He did it; she laid her head on his shoulder.

A huge wave of feeling rose up in him. It startled him; it seemed to have its own force. He held her very tight.

"Kenny..."

She said, "You're the only person I've ever known...who reminds me of my brother."

"Your older brother?"

"Yeah... His name was Scott. He was a gentle, nice person like you. Amazing, because, we didn't grow up with gentleness or niceness or anything good. But that's how he was. You felt... like you could be yourself around him, and it was fine."

"Well. You've got the memory of him at least."

"I do. But it's too painful."

"Well, that I can understand."

"I can't sleep at night."

"I can understand that too."

"It's not only that...it's that and other things."

"Things that you don't want to tell me."

"Not now. Not yet."

"It's all right. It's all right, Colleen."

He wanted to say something else to her, something about the huge feeling in him, but he couldn't.

"Kenny."

"Yeah."

"What did you do with Celeste?"

"Do with her?"

"Yeah."

"Well…everything."

"You did everything with her?"

"Yes."

"How long were you with her?"

"Well, I think it was three months…. Less than that. It was less than three months."

"You did everything with her, and it was less than three months?"

"Yup."

"So why"—she shifted her head on his shoulder—"didn't it last longer."

"Well…I was on the JV basketball team, like I mentioned last night. She was a cheerleader, one of our team's cheerleaders…and that's how it got going. I wasn't a starter, but I came off the bench and got quite a lot of playing time. This guy Wayne Testo, he was in eleventh grade last year, and he was a starting guard on the varsity, I'd say third or fourth best player in the school. And I think it just bothered him that a guy like me, a second-string JV player, had someone like Celeste. She's in my grade, but she's…she's considered, you know…real hot stuff. So he starts flirting with her. At first I didn't think anything of it. I thought, you know, what does it matter, she's with me. But before long…she's with him."

"Oh Kenny that's…that must have been so hard."

"Well, yeah, it was for a while, but…what can I say. I got over it."

"Celeste must be a very stupid person."

"Well…stupid, I don't know. I mean she gets good grades. But…yeah, she's kind of shallow."

She said, "Kenny… What you need is a girl who appreciates you. You don't need a girl like Celeste who's shallow. And you don't need a girl like me who's too screwed up."

"Don't worry about that, Colleen."

"About what?"

"About being screwed up. And you don't have to put yourself down like that. You don't have to say you're screwed up."

"Oh Kenny. If you knew me better, you'd know that I do have to say it."

She lifted her head from his shoulder, leaned it back against the trunk again, gazed forward drowsily.

She said, "Just looks…so perfect."

"It does."

"You know, the big picture, it looks perfect. It's because you can't see the individual people and all the shit they're going through."

"That's true, unfortunately."

"Kenny. We just met last night. I sort of can't believe it. It seems like much longer ago than that."

"Yeah, I know what you mean."

"It's weird, isn't it?"

"It's strange."

She said, "Kenny you know, I'm so tired because, as usual I couldn't sleep at night. Then in the morning, just about when I usually do fall asleep, they start going at it, you know, my mother and the jerk, and then the jerk has his orgasm. And then I couldn't fall asleep after that either."

44

"Did you sleep at all?"

"I was reading for a while. This book *Siddhartha* that my friend gave me. It's actually about a guy who goes off in the woods by himself. It's pretty good. I think I might have fallen asleep, you know, about nine or something, and slept maybe two hours."

"So you must be real, real tired."

"Yes."

She nestled her head, slowly and softly, on his shoulder again.

He hugged her to him.

He ran his fingers through her hair. He did it a bit crazily, clutching clumps of her hair, then smoothing them down ardently. He felt the words *I love you* rise up in him, realized that it was crazy and didn't say them.

She said, "Mmm. Keep doing that."

He did it—now in long, steady strokes—until he heard her breathing evenly and realized she was asleep.

As the boat floated up to the dock again, dusk was already a presence; a faint grey, a deeper stillness. There were still some people on the beach. The boat bumped dumbly into the dock; he grabbed the pile, lifted the rope from the floor of the boat, climbed onto the dock so he could tie it around the pile.

Colleen, still sitting on her seat, said, "Kenny, what time is it?"

"It's…twenty to six."

"Twenty to six. I swore to them I'd be back by five."

"Well. Promises promises."

He offered his hand to help her onto the dock.

"This looks scary."

"Why?"

"Like I'm going to fall in."

"Come on."

"Kenny. Really. I'm scared."

"Colleen. There aren't four feet of water here."

"OK. But you have to jump in after me if I fall."

"OK. I promise."

"Promise?"

"Yeah."

"You'd probably like it anyway." She was giving him a coy, affectionate look.

"Colleen. Come on."

Clutching his hand, she took a big, shaky step onto the dock; then—holding both his hands—another one.

She gave a little squeal as her other leg came onto the dock and the boat moved back a little.

They stood there holding each other's hands.

"Kenny. They're going to be real mad."

"Who?"

"My mother and the jerk."

"Mad? Why?"

"Because I'm late."

"Because you're getting home a little late?"

"They have this thing about supper at five."

"Supper at five?"

"Yeah."

"What difference does it make, supper at five, supper at six?"

"It's just something the jerk has, Kenny, supper at five. He's a weird guy with all kinds of quirks. But the thing is, he's not really that fanatic about it. But now my mother's picked it up from him. *She's* fanatic about it, so His Majesty won't be displeased in any way."

"If I'd have known, I'd have woken you up sooner."

"That's OK."

"You were sleeping so peacefully. You told me you'd hardly—"

"Kenny really that's OK. You don't have to feel sorry for that."

They stood there, facing each other, still holding each other's hands.

He pulled her toward him.

She collapsed into him; they hugged.

"Kenny," she said.

She drew back from him, until they were still holding each other's hands but not tightly.

She said, "I can't be what you want me to be. I'm too messed up."

He said, "Why don't you stop talking about yourself. Just...just go with it. You know?"

She said, "I really should be getting back there."

He looked at her in the grey light.

"So we'll take the boat out again tomorrow?"

"I don't think so. They're going to be so mad about me being late, I don't think I can ask them for that. Not two days in a row."

He looked at her.

"So let's meet at the beach again in the evening."

"OK. We can do that."

"What time do you want to do it?"

"I don't know. Eight?"

"OK."

He said, "We're talking about tomorrow evening."

"Right."

He said, "I'll miss you."

"Kenny. It was so, so nice there today. Thanks. But we really should start walking up."

They parted outside their two bungalows. They'd said little on the way up to them. He hadn't tried to touch her again.

He walked up to his bungalow staring solemnly at the ground.

When he entered it, they were sitting at the dining room table. They were in the latter stages of the meal—not much food left on plates, much disarray on the table.

"Well!" his mother said.

"Well!" his father said. "The mariner returns!"

"Yup," he said.

He went into the bungalow's small bathroom; walked back out toward the table.

"Kept the pot roast hot for you," his mother said, setting a plate on his placemat and sitting down.

"Thanks."

As he was pulling back his chair, pondering the pot roast, rice, and broccoli on his plate, there was sharp shouting from the bungalow next to theirs, bungalow 8.

He stopped. There was a man's voice and female voices.

He waited. It seemed to have ceased.

He sank into his chair.

"That your friend?" his father said.

"Yeah."

"How old did you say she was?"

"She's, uh…going into eleventh, like me."

"Then what are they so mad about?"

"I don't know, they're—"

There was another volley, sharper and fiercer than the first one; a door slammed.

He sat there; he sunk his forehead into his hand.

"What's going on there?" his mother said.

"I don't know, her parents they're kind of...kind of...really difficult people."

Again he waited; now it really seemed to have stopped.

He stared at his food, slowly started eating it.

His father said, "So where'd you go?"

"Oh, we went—you know that island down to the south?"

"*That* island?"

"Yeah."

"That's way out in the lake. You *went* to it?"

"Yeah. It's nice there."

"Well!" his mother said. "Romantic!"

Lizzie, across the table, was looking at him.

"Kenny's in love with that girl."

"Hey you, be quiet."

"No, why don't you be quiet."

"Kids," his mother said. "Talk nicely to each other."

In his room, he lay back on his bed.

The dusk hour outside; a couple of birds singing lazily, as if it were an afterthought.

He saw her hips and stomach as she lay back in the boat; imagined running his hands along the smooth surface, slipping his fingers under her shirt and moving them up, up...

He said, "Damn."

He levered himself off the bed, stepped over to the small chest of drawers where his things were strewn. The book was there—*The Great Gatsby* by F. Scott Fitzgerald. Before the trip, he'd asked his father if he could give him a book, something he could read while they were up there, and he'd given him *The Great Gatsby*.

He'd tried reading it a few times, and he always had two reactions. One was that it was a good, interesting book and he should keep reading it; the other was that it had nothing to do with him—him and his friends and their world—and he couldn't keep reading it. The second reaction was always stronger.

Should he try reading it again?

No; the same thing would happen.

Maybe he could borrow Colleen's book if she'd finished it. That, he knew, he'd be able to read—because she'd read it. Because her fingers had touched it.

He lay back on the bed again.

His right shoulder ached; he realized it was from her head being on it so long. It had started to hurt while she was sleeping; he'd just let it hurt....

He said, "I love her...."

(Love her? Twenty-four hours ago you were lying here and you didn't know she existed....)

(So what...)

He thought: I cannot wait another twenty-four hours to see her again. Cannot stand it.

He heard the TV in the living room; his parents were watching the news. That meant they'd soon—it was always right after the news—invite him to the Scrabble game. That, at least, was good. He could get out of this damn room; it would distract him.

5

After breakfast—his coffee and a cookie or two—he went back to his room, lay back on his bed again, knotted his fingers behind his head, stared at the ceiling, and tried to figure out how he'd get through the time until the evening.

Footsteps approached his room; a knock on the door.

"Kenny!"

It was Lizzie.

"Yeah?"

"Kenny!"

He scowled; bolted from the bed to the door, opened it.

"*What.*"

"Someone here to see you."

She was looking at him, pink-cheeked, bright-eyed.

"*What?*"

"Someone here to see you."

He scowled; went past her, walked out to the living room. He saw her—standing on the other side of the screen door, wearing the same denim shorts as yesterday and a peach-colored polo shirt open at the throat.

"Hi!" he said.

"Hi."

"Um"—he opened the screen door; his free hand went down and touched her hand—"want to come in?"

"I thought maybe we'd go for a walk."

"Oh…why don't you come in?"

She gave a diffident shrug. "OK."

He glanced at his father, sitting at his table on the porch. "This is my father."

"I know. We've met."

"We've met!" his father said. He leaned back, knotted his fingers behind the fan of curls on his head, gazed grandiosely at Kenny and Colleen. "Colleen and I have met!"

"Good."

He gestured with his hand for her to enter.

"And this is Lizzie. I take it you've met."

"Well, not really," Colleen smiled.

"Colleen, this is Lizzie. Lizzie, this is Colleen."

"Hi," Colleen smiled.

"Hi!" Lizzie said brightly.

He closed the door to his room softly behind him. He took hold of her wrists, looked at her; there were dark circles under her eyes. He kissed her on the lips, letting go of her wrists, clasping her. He kept kissing her, clasping her tight; she responded only gingerly.

They stopped; she plopped down on the bed, sunk her face into both hands.

He stared at her.

She said, "You didn't ask if I wanted to do that."

He said, "Sorry."

He said, "Was that really bad for you?"

"No."

She removed her face from her hands, gave him a dull, harried look.

She said, "We can go for a walk. We don't have to be in here."

He said, "Hell with that."

He said, "Don't worry about it, Colleen."

He, too, plopped down on the bed—but not too close to her; he hugged his knees and leaned back against the wall.

He looked at her. She kept sitting there glumly.

He said, "Did you sleep?"

"No."

He said, "I heard that when you got back."

"Oh, that."

She said, "Fucking bitch of a woman. I'd stab her with a knife if you couldn't go to jail for it."

He said, "What did she do?"

"Oh, uh… 'What were you doing with that boy, Colleen? Got a little delayed with that boyfriend of yours?'"

He sighed.

"That's a pain in the ass."

She said, "Your father seems nice."

"Yeah, he is. My mom's OK too. She's not here, she drove into town."

"You cannot imagine for one minute, Kenny, how lucky you are."

"I'm sure that's true, Colleen…. I'm sure that's true. What can I say?"

She turned and looked at him, dull-eyed.

She said, "Got something to tell you."

"What."

She said, "The jerk planned a little trip for Saturday-Sunday. Montreal. His heart's desire is Montreal now.

Another hot noisy city in the middle of summer. But what the hell. That's the ruling."

"So...you'll be gone?"

"I begged my mother to let me stay here for the two days, but, you know...forget it. She's sure I'll turn the place into a whorehouse."

He stared glumly forward.

"Well when will you get back on Sunday?"

"Don't know Kenny. We have to leave some motel up there in the morning, but when the jerk goes on a trip he gets inspired, starts taking all these little detours so he can discover all kinds of wonderful new places. Don't know when we'll be back on Sunday. Might not be till the evening."

"Jesus..."

He moved down toward her on the bed; took her hand and held it. Her hand stayed limp.

"Then on Monday we have to leave here by eleven."

He sighed. "So we've got...not much time. Today and tomorrow really."

"Unless...we get back earlier on Sunday, but I wouldn't count on it."

"We can at least take the boat out tomorrow. Can't we?"

"Yeah I think so. Maybe take it earlier this time. Or maybe just not tell them and take it. Fuck them."

She said, "Did you ever hear of Banford College?"

"Banford College. No."

Because her hand, in his, stayed limp, with no response, he let go of it; went back to leaning against the wall, hugging his knees. She continued to sit as she'd been sitting—at the edge of the bed, looking down at the floor.

"It's this college in Massachusetts. My best friend's sister's a senior there now. She really likes it. It's up on the coast, about as far north in Massachusetts as you can get. Right next to the ocean. It's where I want to go in two years. Best thing is that it's far away from those people—far enough that they can't just hop in a car and see me whenever they feel like it. California would be even better. Alaska. But of course they're not going to pay for that, all those plane rides."

"I've never heard of this place. I can see why you want to go there."

"It might surprise you but I'm a good student."

"That doesn't surprise me at all."

"I work hard so I can, you know, fulfill my dream, which is to finally get out of that place and never go back, except maybe for short visits."

"Well, I can understand that."

"Kenny, the real reason I wanted to talk to you this morning is—if you want to know about all this stuff, all this crap that happened to me, this might be the time for it. Then tonight, when we sit out by the lake, we don't have to talk about it, it can just be nice."

He sat pensively.

"Well, yeah, I do want to know about you."

He said, "Not if it's too unpleasant for you."

"It's all right Kenny. It's all right."

She sat very still.

She took a deep breath.

"You may have thought...where's my father in all this. Well, he's nowhere. He left my mother when I was three. It was very soon after Billy was born. Scott was eight. He took off. He's in Colorado now. Runs a big real estate agency, real successful. Remarried, three kids..."

"Is he in touch with you?"

"Hardly at all, Kenny."

She said, "I think he sees us as sort of people from the other side of the tracks that he's ashamed of. Bad for business. My so-called brother and two sisters out there…I've seen them a couple of times in my life."

She said, "They all came for Scott's funeral. It was like… they didn't think he was worth getting to know while he was alive, but once he's dead, you know, you have to put on these fancy clothes…."

She sunk her head deep into her hands.

He moved down on the bed again, put his arm around her. It was almost like holding something lifeless; there was no response.

"My mother…she's kind of a nymphomaniac. She started bringing these men home almost right after my father left. Some I guess you could call boyfriends. Some were probably just—you know, casual. I was already hearing all kinds of noises. I knew more about sex by the time I was five than a lot of people know when they're fifteen."

She said, "You might wonder how I could live this way. The answer is Scott. He was a big brother. He was always nice. He just…glowed."

A sob shook her; then another; then it came in a silent torrent. He hugged and kissed her almost insanely, also tear-streaked.

She breathed deeply several times as it subsided.

"Colleen…you don't have to go on. It's enough. I get the picture."

She shook her head.

"There's more Kenny."

She breathed deeply a few more times. He kept holding her but her body remained limp.

She said, "Before the jerk my mother had a boyfriend for a couple years. My mother works as a secretary for a shipping company. This guy was some kind of manager there. He was supposedly divorced, but now I think he was just separated or maybe not even that, maybe still with his wife. He fancied himself a great chef. He started coming to our house so he could whip up these supposedly marvelous meals. I was assigned—I was assigned, by that wonderful woman—to be his assistant."

In the silence they heard the car pull up on the gravel; heard his mother shut the car door, walk on the gravel.

"And so while I was assisting the great chef, my mother was usually upstairs, or maybe in the living room—the queen waiting for the great meal to be ready."

She said, "He touched me in all kinds of places."

"Oh God, Colleen."

"Started when I was not yet thirteen, lasted almost a year. Till she got rid of him, so she could move on to the next idiot."

He said, "You didn't tell her?"

"No."

She said, "She wouldn't have believed me. She'd have said I was making it up. Then…then I really might have killed her."

He said, "Scott?"

"He was at Fort Bragg already, officers' training, then he was in 'Nam. I didn't want to burden him with it. I really thought he had enough to deal with."

She said, "So. Now there are two people in the world who know about it."

"Who's the other?"

"Rita. My best friend."

She said, "I can't do anything with guys. I've never had a boyfriend."

They both sat glumly, he still with his arm around her.

He said, "Have you tried…a psychologist?"

She shook her head. "I'm going to ask my mother—and the jerk—to pay for it?"

She said, "My mother would ask what it was for. I'd say I was depressed or something. She'd say 'Snap out of it girl.' She's a jerk. She's an idiot."

"Ask your father."

"Him?"

She said, "The great real estate kingpin out there? I don't think so."

"Just ask him for it. Fuck 'im."

"I don't think so Kenny."

She said, "Why should I do that when I have Rita for a shrink."

"*What?*"

"That's the last chapter of the story Kenny. This last school year she had an idea. It was such a stupid idea that..." She gave a constricted sigh. "I probably shouldn't even be friends with her anymore. But. I forgave her. I guess...you could say that she wanted to help. In her stupid way."

She said, "She thought...maybe if I could do something with a guy, like, in a casual way, I'd see it wasn't so bad, and I could get over it. So..."

She sighed deeply. "She has an aunt and uncle in New Brunswick. That's where Rutgers is, the university. She said—let's go stay with them. Let's pick up a couple of Rutgers guys, guys who won't be too bad because they're college guys. Then you'll see that it's OK. Then you'll be able to get over it."

She sat hunched within herself, small, eyes trained on the floor, obtuse to his nearness.

She said, "So we did it."

She said, "Went to some bar on a Friday night where the college kids hang out."

He said, "So. I guess it wasn't a great success."

"Kenny, I don't think you know what it is just to be a body to someone. I don't think girls ever subject guys to that."

She said, "I know, it was just supposed to be a one-night stand, I agreed to it, I brought it on myself, blah blah.... Just biting a person like an animal. It's sickening."

They sat there in silence; his arm around her, her body limp.

She said, "Kenny I have to get back."

At last she dropped her hand down, rested it on the cloth of his shorts.

She said, "I didn't tell them when I went out. My mother probably thinks I've drowned myself in the lake by now."

"Colleen, I don't even like to hear you talking that way."

She sat very still.

Using her hand that was on his thigh as a lever, she slowly, strenuously stood up.

He stood up, faced her, lightly held her forearms.

She said, "I look like a wreck, right?"

"You look like you were upset about something. So what. People get upset about things sometimes."

He said, "Colleen, know what my sister said yesterday at the supper table?"

"What did she say?"

"She said, 'Kenny's in love with that girl.'"

She looked away from him, toward the floor.

"Kenny I can't do it. I'm too messed up."

She said, "I better get going."

"Down by the lake this evening?"

"Yeah."

In the afternoon he went down to the beach. It was relatively dense with people now; it was Thursday, and with the weekend looming more families were coming to stay at the bungalows. His mother and Lizzie were there; so were Colleen's stepfather, mother, and brother. Her mother had short, dark, curly hair, wore sunglasses, and had a dour look; her body was scrawny, and he found himself wondering why so many men seemed to have been interested in her. There was also a young, blond, French Canadian couple; the woman wore a tiny bikini of a dark, leopard-skin-type material. The bottom part of the bikini consisted of a small, diamond-shaped patch of cloth in front and an only slightly larger, diamond-shaped patch of cloth in back, connected to each other by a sort of webbing. Everyone stared, and some people scowled—including a few of the men, since there were notions of propriety. Kenny looked at it and then found that he had to stop looking. Instead he swam out— way out—beyond the raft, turned over on his back and floated, sighing deeply, staring up at the shining blue.

6

Again he walked to the door as they were getting ready to play Scrabble. He paused with his hand on the doorknob, turned and said, "I'll be going down to the beach to hang around a little with Colleen."

"Oh, rats," his father said. "There goes some of my toughest competition."

"Not sure when I'll be back, but don't worry about it. Might be a little later than the other time."

"Not rowing out to that island again, are you?" his father said.

"Nah," he grinned. "In the dark? I don't think so."

"Well!" his mother said. "Looks like you and that girl are getting along after all."

"Yeah, I guess so."

"Kenny gets along with that girl *real* well," said Lizzie.

"Well, I don't know about that," he said. "Goodnight."

Outside there was a very subtle change in the air, the first hint of autumn. It was just a touch cooler. There was something just faintly sharper in the pine smell. The moon, risen over the hills on the eastern side of the lake, now looked truly full, apparently not yet having been at that point when he'd seen it two nights earlier. Now it was a stunning sphere that looked as if you could reach out and touch it.

As he approached the beach, he was aware that it was some minutes after eight; he hadn't wanted to come on time again, to be the one who always came on time and waited for her. It appeared to have paid off; he saw her dark form, already there in a chair, and with another chair beside her on her left— just where he'd sat two nights ago.

"Well," he said.

She jumped.

"*Kenny.* God, you scared me."

"Sorry."

"You walk up, you know, like some cat, I had no idea you were there."

"Sorry."

She stood up, and they hugged, her head in his chest.

"I'm glad," he said, "you were hospitable."

"Pulled up a chair for you?"

"Yeah."

"Well, look what else I brought."

She gestured, and he peered.

"What's that, a blanket?"

"Yeah. I thought, you know, in case we get uncomfortable in these chairs—in case *you* get uncomfortable, because I know you don't like them—we can sit there instead."

"Great."

Again the bright bar of moon in the lake entranced him. He looked from it to the moon itself, then back at the long silvery bar, as if trying to understand how the one caused the other.

"Love this season," he said.

She looked at him. "What, the summer?"

"No, I mean…August like this, when it's just, just starting to be fall for the first time."

"Yeah."

She said, "It's like…there's something in the air."

"Something that says…look out. September's on the way."

"Yup."

He said, "Feeling any better than before?"

"Better than before… Maybe. Kenny, I never feel that good."

"Get some sleep?"

She sighed. "A little. In the afternoon, when they all came down here. Had a couple of hours of quiet."

"Yeah, I saw them."

"You were down here?"

"Yeah, I wanted to do some swimming, just…stretch out a little."

"When they came back the jerk couldn't stop talking about some Canadian woman in a bikini."

"Oh, her."

"You saw her too?"

"Yeah."

She turned and held him in her gaze.

"Well," she said, "you must be hot and horny."

"Oh, I don't know.… I mean, I generally am."

"Yeah… Yeah, I'm aware of that."

They both sat quiet.

She said, "You know what? We're always talking about me and my problems. So. Let's find out about you for a change."

"Me?" He shrugged. "What do you want to know?"

"Your parents are different religions?"

"Yeah. But they're both unreligious, so it's not any kind of problem."

"The Jews worship God, but not Jesus, right?"

"Yeah, something like that. But my father doesn't do much worshipping. He really cares about Israel, though. He follows it kind of fanatically in the news. I'm supposed to go there next summer."

She stared at him. "*You're* supposed to go there?"

"Yup. Kibbutz volunteer. Work on a kibbutz for a couple of weeks."

"Those kibbutzes…what are they, sort of farms?"

"Sort of. Socialist farms. Everybody shares the work together, everybody's supposed to be equal."

"That's what you're going to be doing for a couple of weeks? Farm work?"

"Yup."

"Ha, ha," she said. "I can't really see you doing farm work."

"Well, it should be an adventure."

"Yeah, I'm sure. Isn't it kind of dangerous there?"

"Not really. Maybe when there's a war. Most of the time there isn't a war. You think there's always a war there, because when there's a war it's on TV. So you think that's how it always is."

She said, "Bet there'll be girls on your kibbutz."

"Yeah. I would think so."

"Those Israeli girls are really beautiful."

"Yeah, they are…. But these days I'm only thinking about one girl."

She sat silently.

She said, "A girl who's going back to New Jersey in a couple of days."

"Well. It's not the other end of the world."

She said, "Can we not talk about this now?"

"OK. But when we are going to talk about it?"

"Tomorrow. I just want it to be nice now."

"OK."

She said, "So your father's a writer?"

"That's right."

"What's your mother?"

"She's principal of a girls' school in Schenectady."

"*Principal.* Pretty good."

She said, "This principal and this writer. They get along?"

"Yeah. Far as I can tell."

"Those are pretty different kinds of work."

"They are. Just like they have different religions. But, I don't know, they seem like a good match."

"A good match. How?"

"My father's impractical. My mother's practical. So they balance each other out."

"How'd they meet?"

"New York City. City College of New York, they were both graduate students there. My mother grew up in Connecticut. My father's family were refugees."

"*Refugees.*"

"Yeah. They escaped from Germany in 1938, when my father was ten."

"Escaped?"

"Yeah. Jews were already in a lot of trouble in Germany by then."

"What would have happened if they'd stayed?"

"They'd have been killed."

"All of them?"

"Yeah, of course. My father's relatives who stayed were killed."

"How many people are you talking about?"

"His aunt, his uncle, their two sons. Four people."

"They were killed?"

"Yes."

She sat there motionless.

She said, after a while, "So much awful stuff goes on."

"Yeah, it does."

After some more time, she said, "You know when I said before that I never feel good?"

"Yeah."

"Well. When we were on the island…I felt good."

"Yeah. That was a nice place."

"It was like we went somewhere else."

"Yeah. It was. It was like being in a different world for a couple of hours."

He said, "We can go there again tomorrow."

"Yup."

"Might be a little hard to get a boat tomorrow though. With all these people who are here now."

He said, "Know what my father said when I told them I was going down here?"

"Nope. What'd he say?"

"He said, 'You're not going to row that boat out to that island again, are you?'"

"What, at night?"

"Yeah."

"No. I don't think so."

"Imagine what that would be like."

She looked at him. "What. Rowing out there in the dark?"

"Yeah."

"I don't think you'd find your way."

"Probably could. It's not really that dark out. With the full moon."

He said, "But. With you not knowing how to swim."

"Me not knowing how to swim?"

He looked at her. "That's what you said. You said you don't know how to swim."

"Oh, yeah. I did say that. Of course I know how to swim."

"Then, uh…why did you say you didn't?"

"I don't know. I was just fooling around."

"Fooling around."

"Yup."

"Fooling—around. Very, very bad Colleen."

"Well, what can I say. Sometimes I'm kind of bad."

He said, after a while, "So, if we both know how to swim…"

"Then…what. Row out to the island?"

"Yeah."

"Kenny, are you nuts? I mean have you really lost it?"

"Why do you say that?"

"Come on."

"We could get there in half an hour. Hang around for a while, another half hour to get back. Still be back not much later than midnight."

"Yeah, and my mother will make sure half the cops in the county are giving us a welcoming committee on the shore."

"Ha, ha."

"Really, Kenny, I mean, forget it, OK?"

"What can I say."

He said, "Well, maybe next summer we can camp out on it."

"Camp out on it."

"Yeah. You were talking about it while we were there. People do it on islands in Lake George. I'm not sure about this lake. For this lake we can be the pioneers."

"Yeah, and if you think my mother and the jerk would let me camp out with a guy, you really really don't know them. Not to mention we're not even going to be here next summer."

"No?"

"We don't exactly come here every summer like you do. This is the first time. My mother doesn't even like it."

"Why not?"

"I don't know. Beach is too small. Too many dogs on the beach. Something like that, who knows."

They both sat quiet for a while.

He said, "Bet that water is a beautiful temperature right now."

He said, "Wish I'd brought a bathing suit."

She said, "Well, I definitely didn't bring one. And you better not get any ideas."

"Ha, ha."

He said, "Be nice to wade in it at least."

"Sir, if wading in the water is what you desire to do, why don't you go ahead and do it."

"Think I will."

The temperature was indeed perfect, the same as the faintly cool air. He walked, feeling the hard sand of the bottom with his feet. He saw the raft, rocking gently by itself.

He called out to her, "This is great."

"Glad you're having fun."

"Madam, why don't you join me?"

"Because I'm worried about you."

"Worried about *me*?"

"Yeah."

He walked a little more, curling his toes to make the sand ooze up between them.

He said, "Madam, your safety is guaranteed."

"Well, it better be."

He saw her, in silhouette, lean over to take off her sandals; saw her dark form walk up to the water.

"Bathtub," she said, stepping in.

"Even nicer."

The water sloshed before her as she waded up to where he was. She stopped a few feet away, oblique to him, not facing him.

"How is it?" he said.

"Nice. Really nice."

"Yup."

He said, "Think about you all the time Colleen."

He said, "Never felt like this before about anyone."

She reached out her hand and put it in his.

He very gently drew her to him, taking her other hand, until they were facing each other.

He said, "So pretty, Colleen."

He said, "Can I kiss you on the lips?"

"OK."

They did it; she still held back. He tried to put his tongue in, but couldn't.

He said, "Colleen. I am not like the other ones. I'm completely different from them. I really care about you."

"Do you listen to me?"

"What?"

"Do you listen to me?"

"Yes of course I listen to you. What are you talking about?"

"Colleen," he said.

He hugged her; put his hands inside her shirt, ran them in long caresses over her back.

"Is this OK?"

"Yes."

"Colleen," he said. "Why don't we go lie on that blanket. We'll hold each other. We'll just...whatever happens happens. If something starts happening and you don't want it to happen, you'll just say so and it'll stop right away. And you know that."

"That woman really got to you."

"What?"

"I can feel it, Kenny."

"Colleen. It has nothing to do with that."

"Nothing?"

"Colleen. That is not what this is about. It's not what this is about."

He said, "Colleen. What did you bring that blanket down here for?"

"So we could sit comfortably."

"If that's what you want to do—if you decide that that's what you want to do—that is what we'll do."

7

This time he heard his mother and Lizzie sitting down for break-fast, and he went out to join them. Not because he wanted to be with them in particular, but to break the monotony of lying there—almost without sleep—for so long.

At the table he surrounded himself with tiredness and silence, managing to ward off the questions they asked him and to discourage further questions. He ate the grapefruit, cereal, eggs, and toast, and drank the coffee, willingly—not because he was hungry in particular but because it was something to do, a distraction. Amid the pauses in the halting conversation, they heard his father's typewriter clattering on the porch.

And back in his room, fingers knotted behind his head, staring at the ceiling.

With a grim feeling—not a celebratory feeling, even though it had happened.

Grim because too much silence.

Too much silence after it; they'd lain on the blanket, and when he held her she'd merely allowed it—again, limply.

Almost dead silence when they went back up the plank steps to the bungalows.

Crickets in the August night, and otherwise—between them—dead, wordless silence.

The tersest arrangements possible when they turned to face each other—deciding to meet at the dock at two the next day.

The faintest goodbye-kiss possible.

And it had been like that during it too. She had been detached from it; allowing things to happen, sometimes taking part in them but more often not; with him borne along even though he knew it wasn't as it should be, thinking she would put a stop to it at some point; then finding himself incredibly at the end of it, stifling his voice in the blanket as his body shook....

Lying now on his back in the stillness that seemed to have pervaded and put a final seal on everything.

And again, footsteps approaching his room.

And a knock on his door.

"Kenny."

"What."

"Kenny."

"*What.*"

"Someone"—Lizzie opened the door a few inches and peered around it—"here to see you."

But when he went out there, it wasn't Colleen standing on the other side of the screen door, but her little brother. Darkly tanned, small, grave.

"Hi."

"Hi. Uh, Colleen," he pronounced, as if mustering courage, "wants to talk to yuh. She's down at the dock."

"Down at the dock?"

"Yuh."

He saw her sitting there at the shallow end of the dock. Wearing a navy blue T-shirt and jeans, her feet in the water, sandals nearby in the sand. She was idly stirring up water with her feet, looking at the bubbly results with idle interest. She almost didn't seem aware of his approach; she glanced up once and seemed to register it with near-apathy.

Still early, but there were already some people at the beach; the drone of a motorboat from out on the lake.

He stopped in the sand, folded his arms, looked at her.

He said, "Hi."

"Hi."

"How you feeling?"

"Oh, wonderful."

She said, "Bet you are too."

"Well, I'm not sure about that."

"No?"

She said, "Why not?"

"I don't know. Couldn't sleep."

"Oh."

She said, "That can be quite a problem."

She sat there stirring up water—a little more intensely— looking down at the results.

He said, "You OK?"

"*OK.* Why shouldn't I be OK?"

"I don't know. You seemed…kind of quiet last night."

Now slowly she looked up at him, with something cold in her gaze he hadn't seen before.

She said, "You got pretty excited."

"Colleen."

She waited, gazing down at the water again.

"Colleen. I asked if that's what you wanted to do."

"Oh, you asked."

She said, "I don't call it that. I call it pressure."

"Pressure."

"Yeah. Pressure."

"Colleen. It's part of what I felt. Part of what I feel."

"What *you* feel. What about what I feel?"

He stared at her.

"Colleen. Who can tell what the hell you feel?"

"Who can tell what the hell I feel." She swirled her feet in the water now, intensely. "Who can tell what the hell I feel."

She said, "Didn't spill out my guts to you, Kenny? Didn't tell you something I only told to one other person in the world?"

"Colleen. Yeah, you did. And the difference between that and me is that I really care about you."

"If you really care about me why don't you listen to me?"

"I don't know what this business is with listening to you. I don't know what you're talking about when you say that. I listen to everything you say."

"Oh do you?"

She stood up now and faced him.

"Did you listen all the times I told you that I don't do that, I can't do that, I'm not the right person for it? Were you listening? At all? When I said that?"

"Yeah I was. And I was listening to other things you said, too."

"Other things."

"Yeah. You flirted with me, Colleen."

"*Flirted* with you."

"Yeah. Flirted. Come on, Colleen. 'If I drown in the lake, will you save me?' 'Wouldn't you like to catch me if I fall off the dock?' And lying back in the boat like that? Come on, Colleen."

"Really sorry I lay back in the boat. I know that might be just too much for someone."

"Colleen."

She held him in her gaze.

"Yeah, OK, Kenny, maybe I flirted a couple of times. I'm a confused person. Do you know that?"

"Yeah I do know that. And you confused me."

"*Confused* you. For every time I did something like that—dared to be just a little flirty—how many times did I tell you other things? That I'm screwed up. Messed up. Fucked up. That I can't handle that kind of thing. How many times did I say that, Kenny?"

"Right. And nobody made you do anything."

"Oh come on Kenny. Constant pressure isn't making someone do something?"

"It's not 'constant pressure' when I keep saying that if you want something to stop, it'll stop."

"OK, you said that. I'll testify to it. You said it. And what if, at the same time you're saying that, you make me feel that I don't have a choice."

"Colleen."

"Damn it," he said.

"It's nature. You can't have that kind of closeness with someone and keep nature out of it. You can't."

"Nature," she said.

"You know what nature is to me?"

Her voice cracked; she stopped. She waited; she wiped a tear from her left cheek.

"Nature to me…is the island. That—"

She stopped again.

"That's how I wanted it to be. Like it was on the island."

"Colleen."

He said, "I can't be Scott. I can't—just be Scott."

She looked at him.

"Nobody—said—you had to be Scott."

He threw up his hands and dropped them to his sides.

"Colleen. We're sitting together. We're holding each other. We're touching each other. You can't—you can't expect—oh, damn it."

"No. I can't expect that your goddamn lust isn't going to get into it."

"Oh, for *Christ's* sake."

"Well you know what, Kenny? I don't want any part of it. You can keep your damn lustful feelings to yourself. You can take a walk in the woods, and think about some slut in a bikini, and cool them off. But don't bring them to me. Because I don't want any part of them. I don't want any part of *you*."

"Colleen."

"No. You listen to me. If somebody says to you over and over and over again, I don't want that, I can't do that, and you can't hear her, and you make her do it anyway, then I don't need you, and I'm finished with you."

He gazed at her in disbelief as she went to her sandals, slipped into them, and walked away on the sand.

She turned around and came back.

"You know why? Because you're all the same. You're all goddamn animals. And *I* don't need it."

She walked away again.

He said, "Col*leen*."

She kept walking. She reached the sandy slope that led up to the steps, started to climb it.

He went and sat on the dock, sunk his head in his hands, clutched his hair until the knuckles turned white.

PART TWO: APRIL 1971

8

Spring in Willowcreek Park. It had been a long time coming, stalled by a winter of bellowing winds and man-high snow-drifts that persisted well into March; but now it was really April, soft and fresh, spring peepers in the ponds, forsythia blooming in the yards. It was night now, and—again, as they had been at night until well into the autumn—the floodlights were on at the outdoor basketball court.

This court and its adjoining tennis court—together known as "the courts"—were part of a sports-pool-clubhouse complex at the entrance to McLendon Estates, a sprawling, rather upscale development. Although most of Kenny's friends lived in the Estates, his family didn't; they lived almost a mile north on Willowcreek Center Road, at an intersection, in an area that was still much more rural than the development, with a small farm across the street. Since he'd been about eleven years old, Kenny had spent a huge amount of time at the basketball court, walking down to it in afternoons and evenings—and sometimes, in summer, even in mornings—with his arm pressing a ball to his side. He had simply fallen in love with the game, everything about it—the feel of the ball, the sound it made on the pavement, the sight (and sound) of it swishing through the net, the incredible fun and drama of it. He spent long hours watching NBA and college games on TV, too. The game became for him what reading books used to be.

Tonight he was in a half-court four-on-four game, which meant a lot of tough jostling and cursing, shots rattling the rim, tussles over rebounds, all in the problematic light of the floodlight, which didn't dispel the dark but only half-invaded it to create a kind of twilight. Kenny—a guard, best at long-range shooting—mostly lingered around the perimeter when his team was on offense, waiting for a space to open and someone to hurl him the ball so he could toss up one of his high, arcing shots that usually swished through. He saw himself as a retiree now. During the winter he'd been on the varsity team, but a benchwarmer; guys who were benchwarmers as juniors almost never made the varsity team as seniors, and he didn't think he would either. Now he was playing the game just for love of it; he had no further hopes of glory. His glory, it turned out, had been being on the varsity team at all; now only the game itself was left.

They were now tied at 9-9, meaning whichever team got two more baskets would win. The star of the other team was Kenny's best friend, Leon. Just tall enough to be a "big man" under the hoop, he made a short fade-away jump shot, and it was 10-9. Kenny's team missed two shots; Leon got the rebound of the second one, flicked the ball to a teammate at the perimeter, who flung it to Benny Wade—also a varsity guard—in the right corner, who hit another jumper and ended the game.

It was nine-thirty on a Tuesday night—a school night—and they all started getting ready to leave.

Kenny found his ball in the grass beside the court, picked it up.

Turning around, he saw Leon facing him.

"Another miserable defeat," Leon said.

"Hey, fuck you," said Kenny. "You guys had Lady Luck on your side the whole game."

"Why don't we walk around a little? I can get us some—" Leon made a motion as if tilting a beer can to his mouth.

"Don't think so."

Leon looked at him. Big and sturdy, he had curly red hair, a merry face with freckles and blue eyes.

He said, "What is it...that girl still?"

Kenny—not looking at him, not at ease—said, "Yeah. Pretty much."

"Gotta get over it."

"Yeah, I know. I thought I had, but...what can I say." He made a gesture, as if trying to say something about the night, the spring, and the mood they put him in.

"From what you told me I don't think she's worth it."

"Leon. She sent her brother to tell me something. That last day. When they were about to leave. She probably wanted to talk to me."

"You don't know that. If she sent him why didn't he come up and knock?"

"He started to but he backed off. He was a shy kid."

"Maybe he wanted to borrow something."

"Yeah, borrow something. They were about to leave. They were throwing their things in their car."

Leon clapped him on the back.

"Don't want to take some medicine for it?"

"Not tonight. Kind of late already. Maybe this weekend."

Lilac was heavy on the air when he turned from Willowcreek Center Road into the driveway of his house. It was a one-story brick house, inhabiting a two-acre yard, facing across Langley Road to the farm. Behind it on one side, the side where his and his sister's rooms were, was a lilac hedge. Each year at this time the scent of the lilacs in blossom, the sound of the peepers, the brightness of the stars had given him ecstasies that he kept secret and didn't think he could communicate to anyone. But this year it was different; they brought back pain he thought he'd put behind him.

Entering the breezeway, he saw that a light was on in the kitchen. To the left were the two rooms—once a garage, converted years ago—belonging to him and to Lizzie; his was in the back, with the lilac hedge behind it. To the right was the kitchen, three steps up from the breezeway. Beyond the kitchen there was a hall with the living room and his parents' bedroom to the right, his father's workroom at the end.

Mounting the steps, he saw his father at the kitchen table, poring over the *New York Times*.

"Hey," his father said absently.

"Hi," he said.

He went past him—past the partition on the left, on one side of which was the dining table where his father now sat, on the other side the kitchen itself.

He opened the refrigerator and peered. He realized that he wasn't sure what he was looking for, or even if he was hungry; he was just acting mechanically, doing what he generally did.

He took a Twinkie from a box, extracted a big can of pineapple-grapefruit juice and poured himself a glass.

He took this snack to the table and sat down across from his father.

His father lowered the paper crisply; looked at him as if just now discovering he was there.

"At the courts?"

"Yeah."

His father kept looking at him.

"Wow."

Kenny looked at him.

He said, "What?"

"You've been in better moods."

"Oh. Yeah, I guess that's true."

He saw that, down past the breezeway and to the left, the light was on in Lizzie's room. He knew that she always tried to overhear conversations.

"Girl?" his father said.

He chewed and swallowed the last of the Twinkie. He said, "You could say that."

"Katie?"

"No. That ended already a couple of months ago."

"Someone new?"

"No… No, actually not so new."

He said, "I'm still thinking about that girl last summer at the lake."

His father, who still had been the holding the *Times* a few inches above the table, now slowly laid it down.

"Marlene?"

"Colleen."

"*Col*leen. Yes."

His father looked intently at him.

"What happened with her, anyway?"

"Oh, well…it's kind of a story."

"Well," his father said. "You know I'm not someone who hates stories."

He smiled. "No, I guess not."

"Well," he said. "It's, uh…it's…I don't know. It started that first night I was too restless to play Scrabble. When I went down to the beach. She was sitting there in a chair."

He paused. Beside and behind the table were two windows, open on the night. The cool air, the lilac scent, drifted in; the peepers sounded more distant and dreamlike.

"And, uh...we started talking. She's from New Jersey. Some small town. They were never at the place, the bungalows, before. This was the first time they were there."

Again he paused.

"Well...she was really depressed.... She told me she could never go down to the beach during the day because her stepfather looked at her too much. She really...she hated her stepfather and her mother. Well, her mother...maybe not hated her totally, but there was hate in it."

He sighed deeply. He slowly drank down the last of the pineapple-grapefruit juice.

"She told me...she told me that her brother got killed in Vietnam."

"He got killed?"

"Yeah, it was a couple of years before."

He said, "She really loved this brother. He was five years older. Name was Scott."

He said, "She was depressed about that, and other things.... She asked me about me a little too. So we had a conversation that lasted a while, and then I told her I had to get going. So...she walked up with me and I asked her if she wanted to go for a rowboat ride the next day and she said that would be OK, but not in the morning because that was her time to sleep since at night she couldn't sleep at all, so it would have to be in the afternoon and I said OK. And then...when we got to the top of the steps I sort of tried to kiss her goodnight, but she didn't let me, she just said 'Goodnight Kenny' or something like that."

He paused. His father was stationary intentness.

"So I asked mom if that meant she didn't like me, and she said, nah, it just meant she wanted to get to know me better, and the fact that she agreed to the rowboat ride was probably a good sign."

He said, "So when we finally pushed off in the rowboat... that was when her mood changed. Her mood got really good... she really liked being out there in the sun, away from everything I think. She was really mad at her stepfather, and her mother...but she also joked about it and she was pretty funny. She got kind of flirty with me. She asked if we could go somewhere instead of just drifting around, and I suggested the island, and she said sure, even though she said she didn't know how to swim. Later it turned out, though, that she did know how to swim, she was just saying that."

Again he paused.

"Colleen," his father said, "sounds pretty complicated."

"Yeah. Complicated. That's for sure."

He said, "She was in a good mood, but she was telling me how much she wanted to commit suicide, how the only reason she didn't do it was her little brother, that kid that was up there with them.... We talked about her stepfather again, and she said it was really bad the way he looked at her. So I asked her if he ever...you know...if he ever touched her. She said no, but there was someone else who did...but she didn't want to talk about it. We were getting closer to the island and she really loved it out there."

He said, "And then, at the island..."

He raised his hands and dropped them.

He sat very still. He stared forward, as if at something that would clarify what he wanted to say.

"I don't know. It was beautiful there.... I tried to get something going with her again, but she still wouldn't let me. Instead we were just sitting against a tree. We were kind of holding each other. I started...I don't know...just to feel things about her...really deep."

He sighed.

"Well, when we rowed back, it was really quiet, it was getting toward evening, and we didn't talk much. She told me her parents—her mother and her stepfather—would get really mad because she was half an hour late or something. So she said she couldn't ask them to go out in the boat again the next day, so we agreed we'd just meet down at the beach in the evening again. And of course...when she went in, the two of them, her mother in particular I think, really got on her case."

"I remember that," his father said.

"Yeah..."

He said, "But the next morning she surprised me, because she came over to visit me while I was in my room."

The door to his parents' bedroom opened. His mother, wearing a nightgown with a robe over it, came walking out to the kitchen.

She stopped in the kitchen.

"Well," she said. "You guys look you're deliberating the fate of the world."

"We are, sweetie," his father said. "And we're going to solve it pretty soon. And once we do, I promise I'll join you."

His mother stared at them a moment longer—seeming to take in that they were having an especially serious talk.

"OK, sweetie," she said. "Goodnight. Feeling OK, Kenny?"

"Yeah, fine, mom, thanks. Goodnight."

When she was back in the bedroom, his father looked at him with the same patient expectancy.

"So," he said. "We were sitting in my room together, and she wanted to tell me about the bad stuff in her life, to get it out of the way, so that in the evening, when we were sitting by the lake, it could just be nice. So…she told me about that other guy…the guy who touched her. It was a boyfriend of her mother's. I think it was the last one, the last boyfriend, before she met the stepfather. He was considered some kind of cook, and he'd cook meals at their house, and her mother would send her to help him. And while she was helping him…she said that he'd touch her all over the place."

His father started intently at him.

"How long did this go on for?"

"I think about a year."

"A year."

"Yeah."

"And how old was Colleen when this was going on?"

"Twelve. And then thirteen."

"Twelve and then thirteen."

He said, "She didn't tell her mother about it?"

"No. She said her mother wouldn't have believed her."

"Has Colleen gone for help? Professional help?"

"No. She said she wouldn't ask her mother and her stepfather to pay for it."

"Is there a father in the picture?"

"Yeah, that's another thing. She told me other things, too, about her life. Her father left them when she was three. He lives in Colorado now, and he's a big success in real estate, but she said he ignores them almost completely. She wouldn't ask him for money either, guess she hates him too."

His father just looked at him.

"So…we got that out of the way. More or less. So we could have a nice time by the lake at night. Supposedly. But… it wasn't that simple."

He said, "So that night Colleen brought a blanket and she spread it out in the sand. She said it was so we could sit comfortably when we got tired of sitting in those chairs, which were pretty uncomfortable. So…we were wading around in the lake, and I asked her if she wanted to go lie on the blanket together. I said that if things started happening, and something happened that she didn't want to happen, she should just say so, and it would stop."

He sighed. He stared out the window that was across from him, into the darkness where the lilac hedge was a vague bulk.

"So, uh…"

He looked around, as if for some sort of help.

"So I had sex with her, on the blanket. It was like…she wasn't really with me, most of the time. Some of the time, actually, she was. Usually not. I really thought she'd say to stop at some point, but…she didn't…. Afterward she was totally quiet, she hardly talked."

He said, "So…the next day her brother came to our door and told me she wanted to talk to me, down by the dock. I went down there. She was just sitting there watching her feet stir up the water as if she didn't even see me. So I said, how you feeling, and she says 'Oh wonderful,' really sarcastically. And then…she starts letting me have it. She said that I forced her into it, that I pressured her into it. I said it wasn't that simple. I said that she flirted with me, and she got really sarcastic about that, then she admitted it was true, but then she said what about all the times she said she was too messed up for that kind of thing, for, you know, really getting going with each other in a serious way. I said that I told her—I told her—to tell me to stop if I started doing anything she didn't want me to do. She said I made her feel she had no choice."

He said, "She said…she said was finished with me, and she walked away. She came back and she said…guys are all animals and they're all the same, and she walked away again. And that was the last time I talked to her."

His father stared at him motionless.

He said, "Colleen is a very troubled girl."

"I don't think…that that's true, that I gave her no choice."

"Of course it's not true. *She* doesn't know what she wants."

They sat silently.

He said, "There's one other thing…that Lizzie told me."

"What did she tell you?"

"Well…when Colleen and I had that scene, by the dock, it was Friday. On Saturday and Sunday Colleen's family went for a trip to Montreal. I knew that they were coming back late on Sunday and leaving, leaving the whole place, on Monday morning…. So Lizzie says that on Monday morning she saw the kid, Colleen's brother, come up to our door again."

While they sat quietly, the door to Lizzie's room opened.

He saw her come out, wearing a long, loose shirt and slippers, to the little foyer outside her and his rooms.

She said, "He didn't come to the door. He just took one step up on the porch."

His father looked at him, wheeled in his chair so he could see Lizzie.

"Lizzie," he said. "Eavesdropping?"

"Nope."

"No?"

"Nope. I just hear you guys. Your voices are hearable."

He said, "You said he came to the door."

"I didn't say that, Kenny. I said he, like, took one step up on the porch, and kept looking at the door, and it was like he turned back."

She said, "It was, like, when they were just getting ready to leave, when they were taking stuff out to their car already."

"So he didn't make it to the door," his father said.

"Nope."

"OK Lizzie. You're dismissed. You better get some sleep."

"Sure. At your service."

She looked at them bright-eyed and went back into her room.

His father turned and looked at him.

He said, in a considerably lower voice, "I might—I might have been able to put the whole thing behind me—if it wasn't for that thing about her brother coming to our place—or trying to come to our place—at the last minute."

"You think he was bringing a message from her?"

"Why else would he come there?"

"So why do you think he turned back?"

"I don't know. He was a shy kid."

He said, "And now…I never even found out her last name. I can sort of remember the name of the town where she lives, Pasamac or something, I could find it on a map. But…I'd like to, you know, write to her, ask what it was she wanted to say, but…I don't even know her last name."

His father said, "Kenny, that isn't a problem."

He looked at him slowly.

"We know the Hogarths, the people who own Pleasant Bay or whatever it's called. Undoubtedly they'll have their address. I could just call them tomorrow."

He sat very still.

His father said, "The question is…if that's what you want to do, if you want to write to her."

He seemed to wait for Kenny to say something; he said nothing.

His father said, "She's a very troubled girl. She's going to stay that way unless she gets some help for this. Even then…

she might or might not get out of it. She might stay that way for a long time. She has a lot—a lot—weighing her down."

He sat very still.

He said, "If I just write to her, it doesn't mean I have to get involved with her again."

"It doesn't have to, but it might."

"I can't stand…I can't stand that it ended so suddenly like that…. If she had something else to say to me, I can't stand that now I don't know what it was."

"Whatever it was, it sounds like it came from confusion. Something at the last minute, when it was almost too late. Or maybe already was too late."

He stared at the table, tapped lightly on it with his fingers.

"I can't…I can't just forget about it. Have to try to get in touch with her again."

9

The next day, when he got home from school, his father told him that the stepfather's name was Ronald Corrigan and gave him their address in Pasamanack. He said Colleen's last name wasn't likely to be Corrigan, but he could write to her there, care of the Corrigan family.

He said "Thanks," took the slip of paper with the address to his room, closed the door, plopped down on his back on the bed.

It was April, but it had been a very warm day, the year's first. In school he'd been even less able than usual to focus on what teachers were saying. It didn't help that he'd hardly slept at night either. He hadn't been able to believe that he'd have her address, that he'd be able to write to her. He'd feared that those people, the Hogarths, had lost it or thrown it away. Now he had it in his hand; his fingers were sweaty. He realized that—lying here on his bed, in his room—he was clutching it as if it might go somewhere. He set it on the night table beside him—but even then he put the lampstand over an edge of it, so a breeze wouldn't waft it away. Looking at it again, he read:

Ronald Corrigan
32 Meadowlark Lane
Pasamanack, NJ

In the evening, after supper, he sat at the desk in his room where—when he felt like it—he did his homework. Before him was an open notebook bathed in lamplight.

Holding a pen, he stared at the page and kept staring. The peepers had already started outside, sweet and silvery. Guys were gathering at the courts.

Why was he doing this? Why not just walk down to the courts and play some basketball? She'd forgotten him already. Well, maybe not forgotten—but she was against him, she hated him, he was the last person she wanted to hear from.

He spent five minutes deciding whether to write "Dear Colleen" or just "Colleen." Finally he wrote "Dear Colleen"; then picked up the pen again and put a comma after it.

He stared at the blank space—the huge blank space—under the two words and the comma. He felt astounded that he was supposed to fill this space with something.

At around ten o'clock, Kenny, for the eleventh time, tore up a notebook page with some writing on it, tossed it into a waste-paper basket beside him.

He crossed his arms on the desk and let his forehead fall on one wrist.

It seemed that—no matter how hard he tried—he couldn't get away from two things he didn't want: either to sound like someone introducing himself in a speech, at some kind of formal dinner, or to sound like someone too ingratiatingly friendly.

He pushed the chair back and stood up. He walked crisply out of his room to the breezeway.

Both his parents were at the kitchen table. They were in the midst of low, intense talking, but he said loudly, "Just taking a walk in the backyard."

He saw his father's face come peering around to look at him. "No basketball tonight?"

"Nope. Got a little too late I guess."

It was lovely out, cool, fragrant, wet with dew. The peepers wove their silvery magic. He walked to where the woodshed—which was behind the lilac hedge—was a bulk to his left, and before him was the stretch of grass that ended in the woods. There were stars and a half-moon over the woods.

He stood there. He was wearing canvas shoes without socks, and the dew soaked right through the soles.

He looked at the stars and the moon. They'd been here while he was writing, or trying to write; they looked completely indifferent, at peace.

Up in the Adirondacks now, the moon was reflected in lakes, and people who lived there all year round—through the winter, when the lakes froze and were covered with snow—were getting bungalows, beaches, and boats ready for vacationers, people who came only in late spring and summer and early fall to splash and make noise and didn't really know the place. Out on Blue Spruce Lake now the water was black and silent as the end—or the beginning—of the world, as if nothing and no one had ever been there but some fish. As if two kids had never been out there in a rowboat last August, two kids who didn't even know each other anymore, who lived in different places with hundreds of miles of night between them.

At two in the morning, after lying stock-still on the bed, hands behind his head, staring at the ceiling, he bolted in a swift movement to the desk (where the lamp was still lit), picked up the pen, and started writing on the notebook page:

Dear Colleen,

Well, guess you'll be surprised to hear from me. I'm still not sure what your last name is! But I kept wanting to write to you—even though it's been a while now—and I talked to my father about it, and he said he could get your address from the people who run the vacation place. So I hope it's OK that I'm writing to you.

I guess the time that we were together, even though it was only a few days, was important to me and made some kind of impression on me. At least, I haven't been able to stop thinking about it. Or maybe I stop for a while, but it comes back. I know we didn't part on good terms. I'm sorry about that—I know that a lot happened very fast and it was confusing, to both of us. I would be happy if we could just be on good terms again instead of there being anger between us. Or if there's anger, I would hope we can communicate about it and see if we could get over it.

Colleen, my sister told me that just as your family was getting ready to leave on that Monday morning, your brother came up to our bungalow and looked like he wanted to say something, before

turning back. I haven't been able to put that aside—
the thought that possibly you wanted to tell me something there at the end but for some reason, maybe
all the confusion, the message didn't get through.
Or maybe there wasn't something like that—maybe
what I'm describing to you sounds like some kind of
crazy fantasy about something that never happened.
But even if so, I would still hope that we can communicate again.

As for how I'm doing—not bad. I was on the
varsity basketball team this year but I hardly got into
games, I was a benchwarmer, and now it looks like
my "official" career is over. But I still love the game—
guess I always will—and I still play a lot just for
fun. Meanwhile there's already talk about applying
to colleges in the fall, and with basketball not what
it used to be (I mean not some kind of "career"), I've
started reading books again quite a lot, like I used
to when I was a kid. I remember, last summer, you
told me you were reading *Siddhartha*. I read one of
Hermann Hesse's books not long ago, *Narcissus* and
Goldmund, and I really loved it. Fortunately I've got
a father who's really good at recommending books
to me!

Well, Colleen, I'd be really happy to hear from you.

Your friend,
Kenny

10

Three weeks later it was still April, but the gold-green leaves of early spring had already deepened to a lush, summery green. On a Friday evening at the courts, there were enough guys there that Kenny was in a full-court five-on-five game. This time Leon was a teammate; Kenny, navigating from the perimeter when he wasn't shooting, fed him crisp passes that Leon—sometimes, since he was up against one of the school's best defensive players—turned into sturdy little bank shots.

It was the last game of the night, and their team won, 11-8. Shuffling off to the courtside to look for his ball, he recalled that he hadn't taken it, since they were supposed to go somewhere after the game.

Leon came up to him with his hands held high, and they did some loud palm-slapping.

"Hey!" Leon said. "Nice goin'. Nice *passing*."

"You got some good hoops off Connors."

"Yeah, Joey's tough. Gotta ram your shoulder into him. Gotta get physical with him if you're gonna get any hoops at all."

"Well, you got some."

"Sooooo," Leon said. "How we doin'?"

Leon stood with his hands on his hips, regarding him. Around them others had formed little knots and were planning places to go. Some were planning to go places in cars—like Leon, who was seventeen now, could drive at night, and had been granted one of his parents' cars for the evening.

He said, "I'm doing great."

Leon looked at him. "Yeah, sure."

"Yeah, what the hell."

"No letter today?"

"Course not."

"So," Leon said. "We picking up the girls?"

"Aa, I don't know."

"You gotta get out of this."

"Yeah. I got to."

Leon kept giving him his blue, watchful gaze.

"One friend to another, OK? OK old pal? This girl has been *nothing* but a pain in the ass to you. *Nothing* but a pain in the ass. You lie with her on a blanket one night and the next day she does nothing but bitch at you. Practically accuses you of raping her. Makes you feel like shit. Makes you feel like shit for what is it…half a year now? More. More than half a year. Then, after all that, you're still nice enough to write to her. Can she even answer? Course not. Fuck 'er."

"She'll answer."

"She will?"

"Yes."

"What is it now, two weeks since you wrote to her?"

"Three weeks."

"*Three* weeks. How long does it take mail to get between here and New Jersey? Two days? Three days? Come on old pal. I don't like seeing you this way. You gotta put her aside."

"Yeah, you're probably right."

"Kenny. Terry is a nice girl. *Really* nice. She wants to meet you."

"OK, so let's go."

They got into the car, which was Leon's parents' lesser car, an old Studebaker. As they pulled away from the courts its headlights swept the grass. Leon edged it into the parking lot of the clubhouse, wormed his way through the parked cars toward the road.

Turning into the road with his left hand, with his right hand Leon opened the glove compartment, took something out, and handed it to him. It turned out to be a flask of vodka.

"Something to make you feel better," Leon said.

Kenny opened it and sipped some.

The car made its way on a long, meandering road of the development.

"OK, so who's this Terry? Tell me again."

"Terry? She's Pam's cousin. Told you about it pal but you're so out of it you don't pick up on things. She's from Rochester. Visiting Pam for the weekend. She's real nice. Told her about you. Said she really wants to meet you."

"Tell her I'm fucked up?"

"No, why would I tell her that. That's not usually my marketing strategy."

Kenny took a bigger swig of the vodka. He sat back, sighed deeply.

He said, "What the hell we doing with them?"

"Oh, that. Official story is—we're taking them to Delgado's. That's what Pam told her parents. Unofficial—to the Lookout."

"The Lookout."

"Yup."

"Why not Delgado's?"

"Come on, man. You need something better than spaghetti. *Even* better."

He said, "Trying to get you out of this, man. This rut that you're in."

"What makes you think this Terry can get me out of the rut?"

"Hey man, who knows. Just thought it's worth a try."

Well into McLendon Estates, they pulled up beside the front lawn of Pam's parents' house. Pam had been Leon's girlfriend for about a year. A dark-haired, big-boned girl, famous for being busty, she was considered yet another of Leon's triumphs.

Each of them opened the door beside him.

Leon stopped, looked at him.

"What the hell you doing."

"What."

"Think I want you walking up there so her parents can, like, smell the vodka distillery on your breath?"

"Oh. OK, what the hell."

"Wait here, man. But when we *do* come out—when we *do* come out—please go to the back seat so the lady can join you. So she won't think it's a goddamn chauffeur service. I mean you gotta be sociable."

"OK. Whatever you say, Leon. It's all…you're in charge."

Sitting there in the dark, he sipped the vodka. He found himself wishing that they wouldn't come out, wouldn't come to the car; that he could just keep sitting here in the dark, with the vodka.

They approached noisily, talking and laughing. He got out, opened the back door, slid swiftly onto the seat. All three of the others opened doors. "*Hey!*" Leon said. "Almost forgot the stowaway here. Looks like he's doing some winetasting for us." "Hi Kenny!" said Pam, climbing in opposite Leon. "Hey, Pam," he said.

To his left, Terry came slowly, diffidently into the car. Light from a streetlight fell on her; she was short, she had long blond hair, high cheekbones, pale grey eyes, and a face that looked at him with a small smile.

"Guess you're Kenny," she said.

"Guess I am. How you doing?"

"Great!"

Pam turned around and looked at him. "I don't think that's wine he's tasting, Leon."

"No?" Leon said. "Whaddya got there, pal, something stronger?"

"Little stronger."

"Gimme a hit on it."

He reached forward to give him the flask. Leon took a good-sized swig. He smacked his lips and sighed grandly; said, "Ladies?"

Pam took a drink from it.

"Yeah, some wine," she said. "What do you think, Terry?"

She reached out and gave her the flask. Terry took a very delicate, hesitant sip.

"Yow!" she said. "I *don't* think it's wine. I think Kenny's indulging in something a little stronger."

She held out the flask to him with long, thin fingers.

He took it and drank from it.

"Yeah, what can I say. Strength is power."

The Lookout was a patch of open grass where cars could park; you got to it by taking a tiny, twisting back road and then a dirt road. Although it was near cliffs that overlooked the Mohawk River, it faced a forest and did not look out on anything, and no one knew how it had gotten its name. For years it had been a place where kids came in cars at night to drink, smoke grass and hash, and have make-out sessions and the like. Since early last fall, fewer had come to it; there had been an incident where the cops raided the spot and made arrests, and two guys who were caught with grass were arraigned and their parents had to pay fines for them. Now, though, with the spring, people were starting to go to the Lookout again.

Tonight as Leon pulled into it, headlights sweeping the grass and the front row of tree trunks, the place was empty. Leon—who, as he drove, had been drinking, left hand holding the steering wheel and right hand the flask—turned the motor off, and they sat, windows open, in the darkness and stillness. From the nearby marshes came trilling and cooing noises.

"So this is the Italian restaurant?" said Terry.

"Yup," said Leon. "You can order...tortellini, linguini, lazarini, whatever the hell you want."

"Terry, don't listen to him," said Kenny. "He's bullshitting you."

"Oh really? I'm disappointed. I really wanted to order the lazarini."

"Terry," said Leon, extending her the flask, "I think you'll have to content yourself with this."

"Uh-oh," said Terry, taking the flask, "he's trying to get me drunk. Kenny, what should I do? I think he's trying to get me drunk."

"You'll just have to fend him off. I mean the guy…he's a freight train when he gets going. You just have to fend him off."

"It's not too hard, Terry," said Pam.

"Well that's good," said Terry. "Here Kenny, I just took a little tiny sip of this, I think there's some left."

Kenny took the flask from her and pretended to scrutinize it; it was still about half full.

"Oh yes," he said. "There are still a few molecules in it."

He took another swig, leaned his head back on the seat, closed his eyes.

"What kind of molecules?" said a voice.

He opened his eyes.

"Huh?"

"What kind of molecules are they?" said Pam.

"Oh. Uh…" He peered at the flask again. "Let's see…let's see…it's uh…vodka oxide."

"Vodka *oxide*," said Pam.

"I didn't know Kenny's a chemist," said Terry.

"Terry, he's a great chemist," said Leon. "We're in ninth-grade science class together, right? This kid did the copper-sulfate experiment the fastest I've ever seen. Two seconds and… boom. Blue crystals. He's like, a magician."

"Don't listen to him," Kenny said. "He's plastered."

"No really, Terry," Leon said, turning and looking at her. "You know how long Kenny and I have been friends? Going back to like…prehistoric times. Before we could read and write. He's hell on wheels. An athlete, real smart, all the girls going after him. The kid's incredible. Always has been."

"You hear that, Kenny?" Terry said. "Your friend's really talking you up."

"Yeah, but you don't know how much I paid him for it."

"Oh, no," Terry said. "*Paid* him for it. I'm so disappointed. I thought you guys were like, honest citizens."

"*These* guys?" said Pam. "Don't think it, Terry."

"Hey Wasserman," said Leon. "Water Man. Gimme a hit on that, will you?"

Kenny—having lost the awareness that he was holding it—stared dumbly at the flask; then held it out to him.

Leon drank from it.

He looked at Pam.

"Pamela, my love."

He said, "Why art thou so far from me?"

"Because," she said, "thou art far from me."

They moved toward each other on the seat; clasped in a long kiss.

They stopped; Leon turned to Kenny.

"Water Man," he said. "You gotta take this off my hands."

He handed Kenny the flask.

They kissed again, longer this time; they began to sink behind the backrest.

"Think the time has come for us to take a moonlit walk, Kenny," said Terry.

He looked at her. "Yeah, think you're right."

Climbing out of the car, he took the flask with him. He didn't want to leave it there, to stop drinking from it.

The moon was high over the woods, shedding a cottony light. The night was full of the banter from the marshes, like a mad orchestra tuning up. As they walked away from the car he put his right arm around her, his left hand holding the stout neck of the flask. When they neared the woods, he stopped, set the flask down on the grass, turned and faced her.

What he could see of her face in the moonlight reminded him of a fish. He put both arms around her, bent down, and kissed her. Her lips and tongue were cool within a warm vapor of vodka.

He moved his head back and looked at her.

"Terry, you know, uh…I'm glad you came with us."

"I'm glad I did too, Kenny."

This time the kiss was longer; he held her to him tightly. He knew what she could feel but didn't care about it.

"Uh…" he said. "Maybe we could be more comfortable if we lie down."

"If we lie down."

"Yup."

"You know what, Kenny?"

"What."

"I don't think so."

"No?"

"Nope."

"Why not."

"Think it's, you know…the grass is all wet. Think it's too wet."

"Well you got your jeans and your jacket."

"I know, but I don't want to get them all wet."

"Hmmm," he said.

He said, "One of those trees probably has a wide trunk. We could sit against one of those trunks. That OK?"

"Yeah, OK."

Sitting against a tree trunk, he encircled her with his right arm and pressed her to him; with his left hand he raised the flask to his lips and sipped from it.

Not far away they could see the bulk of the Studebaker. It was now silent as if no one had ever been in it.

He began running his fingers through her hair.

She pressed her head on his shoulder.

"Mmm," she said. "You do that nicely."

She said, "Did you get training for this?"

"Nope."

"Just know how to do it."

"Yup."

"Mmm…"

He said, "Have you ever been on an island?"

"An *island*?"

"Yup."

"Yeah. I've been on Simcoe Island in Lake Ontario."

"How's that?"

"Nice. Why do you ask?"

"Oh… I was on an island. You know Blue Spruce Lake?"

"In the Adirondacks?"

"Yeah."

"Heard of it. Haven't been there."

"Oh, well, we go there every summer…. Last summer, I went out to this little island with this girl that was there. In a rowboat."

"Yeah?"

"Yeah. Just this really tiny island, but way out in the lake."

"Who was this girl?"

"Oh, just…someone from New Jersey."

"New Jersey."

"Yeah. She just happened to be there with her family. At this vacation place on the lake. Where I and my family were staying."

"Something special about this girl?"

"*Special*. Why do you say that?"

"Well, I mean you're still talking about her. When did you say it was, last summer? That's more than half a year ago."

"Oh... Well, being on the island was special."

"Being on the island with this girl."

"Oh. Well...maybe."

"Sounds like you're still thinking about her."

"Well, not that much."

"Not that much?"

"No."

"Kind of much, I have a feeling."

"Well...maybe."

"So what happened?"

"Oh, it's kind of a long story.... We parted on kind of bad terms. So...I tried writing her a letter."

"When was that?"

"Few weeks ago."

"She answer?"

"Not yet."

"Not yet?"

"Nope."

"Where did you say she lives?"

"New Jersey."

"Well that's not really so far for a letter."

"No."

"I would think that, you know...maybe she still thinks you're on bad terms. Taking her kind of long to answer."

"Yeah, you might be right about that."

They fell silent.

He tried insinuating his finger between her jacket collar and her neck, running it softly along her neck. She didn't stop it, but she didn't respond.

He leaned his head back against the trunk; took a sip from the flask; closed his eyes.

"Terry."

"Yeah?"

"This ground around here? It's pretty dry. I think these roots, you know, they suck up the water."

She felt the ground with her hand.

"Yeah, it's pretty dry. Why, because you want to lie down on it?"

"Be nice, wouldn't it?"

"Well, I don't know, Kenny.... You know, Rochester, it's about four hours from here. And I'm going back on Sunday."

"Yeah, but then...why did you agree to come tonight."

"Oh, you know, all the things Leon was saying about you...I was just curious."

"So, you're disappointed?"

She laughed. "No."

"No?"

"No. I mean I can see that you're nice, you're smart, you're funny. It's just...I don't know. First of all, we're pretty far away from each other. And also...you haven't gotten over this girl."

"Oh, well...I'll get over her."

She laughed again. "You know, Kenny, it's not something I want to bet on. I tried that once.... You know, it was a guy in my school, and I always really liked him, but, like, I could see that he still hadn't gotten over his girlfriend. His former girlfriend. Supposedly. So, like, I said—I'll be able to get him out of that. Great me. But...didn't work. I was with him a couple of months...and then he goes back to her."

"Yeah, but...how will I be able to do that, if she doesn't answer my letter."

"*Kenny*... It's not what she'll do or won't do. It's that... you're still hung up on her. She's still in you."

He took a deep sigh. He drank from the flask.

"So let's just...you know. Let's not try to figure everything out."

"Let's just have a good time, come what may?"

"Yeah."

She chuckled.

"Sorry, Kenny, I'm just not like that. I'm kind of a square. What can I say."

He sat glumly, his eyelids heavy.

"Oh, boy. What the hell."

He lifted the flask and took another drink.

PART THREE: APRIL 1974

11

Usually he liked the bus ride from Binghamton, where he went to the university, to Schenectady. It passed through farm country that was almost forgotten, almost as if from another century. Tourists went to the Adirondacks, to the Catskills; but the rolling hills of central New York State weren't on the tourism map. Passing through them gave him a feeling of calm—and of wonder. Wonder that people still lived this way—on farms, in little shops, going to little diners where the waitress said "What can I getcha" and everyone had known everyone else for years.

And now it was April with a sky of winsome blue, gold-green leaves on the trees, forsythia and magnolia and lilac blooming in the yards of old white houses with wells and red shutters. But for him, now, all of it was only pain—sitting alone toward the back of the bus, not reading, hardly moving, forehead slumped against the window.

At the bus terminal in Schenectady his father—for once grim-faced, not cheerful—strode up to him, and they hugged briefly.

It was a weekday, and his mother was at work, Lizzie in school; but his father, as always, had been home, and able to come and pick him up.

"How you doing?" his father said.

"Not too good."

"No. Who is."

They walked out to the car in the parking lot, Kenny carrying his big cylindrical canvas bag in which he'd tried to throw everything he'd need for a few days. A pleasant spring day in Schenectady—the town not too busy in this weekday mid-morning, low brown buildings against the April blue.

"What time's the funeral?" he said as his father pulled the car out into the street.

"Three. At their church. Mom has to leave work early, Lizzie has to leave school early."

His father, stopping at a light, sitting there, said, "I heard more about it."

"What'd you hear?"

"He was leaving a bar after midnight, and he crashed into an electricity pole. There was another kid in the car, and he was banged up but not too badly. Of course this will be hushed up. Priest probably won't say a word about it."

"Something you can read here," his father said as they went up the steps of the breezeway to the dining table. His father picked up the *Schenectady Gazette* from the table, opened it to a page, folded the page, and gave it to him.

He sat down slowly, holding the paper and staring at the page, while his father went to make coffee.

Leon Hartell (1954-1974)

Leon Hartell, 20, of Willowcreek Park, died Tuesday, April 9, 1974, in Ithaca, New York, where he was a physics major at Cornell University. He was born on March 14, 1954, in Peekskill, New York, and moved with his family to Willowcreek Park in 1964. He attended Willowcreek Park Central School where he graduated magna cum laude in 1972. He is survived by his parents, Ralph and Candace Hartell of Willowcreek Park, his brother, Jason, and his sister, Gwynne.

Services will be held on Thursday from 3 to 5 at the Church of Our Lady on 43 Averill Lane in Willowcreek Park, with Rev. Clifford Hunnicut officiating. Interment will follow at the Paths of Peace Cemetery. Donations may be sent to an Ellis Hospital memorial fund.

As he was staring at it, his father came around the partition holding two cups of coffee, which he set on the table.

"Something to eat?" he said.

"No, that's OK."

He kept staring at the page as the two of them sat there, then picked it up and put it aside.

He said, "He had everything going for him. But he was wild. I don't know why he was so wild."

He said, "All that crazy energy."

"Sometimes, with talented people, it's like that," his father said.

"Somebody so intelligent and…I saw him lots of times, at night, driving a car with one hand on the wheel and the other hand holding a bottle, drinking from the bottle. Just… crazy…"

He said, "I wish I'd told him, you know, in those days, Leon, maybe you shouldn't do that. But I wasn't too bright myself."

"Kenny, he was responsible for himself. Everybody's bright after the fact."

He went into his room, feeling stiff, as if he could hardly direct his hand to open the door. He closed it behind him. The windows—the one that looked out on the side yard and Willowcreek Park Center Road, the one that looked out on the lilac hedge—were open on the spring.

He dropped his bag on the floor. He fell backwards onto his bed like a sack.

The birdsong out there, the scent…

They—he, his parents, Lizzie—would have to put on nice clothes and stand there in the church. They would have to hear the priest. They would have to see Leon's parents, his brother, and his sister, would have to say things to them—at least to the parents. They would have to see a varnished box that had Leon in it. Then they would have to go to the cemetery and see the box lowered into the earth.

Until now he'd been to only one funeral in his life—that of his father's father. It had been in a green, shady cemetery across the Hudson River from Manhattan. It had been a traditional Jewish funeral, meaning that male relatives of his grandfather—including, of course, his father—had had to toss clods of earth onto the coffin with shovels until the coffin was covered with the earth and could no longer be seen. He hadn't been close to this grandfather, who would reminisce to him in a heavy German accent in a way he found hard to follow, hard to connect to.

But his grandfather had been over seventy years old.

Now there was a throng of memories of Leon, going back to when they were both ten. Each memory wanting to get into his mind, each one the sharp point of a knife. It had been like this since Tuesday evening in his dorm room at Binghamton, when both his parents had called him, and his mother had said, "We've got something to tell you. It's not good news." And now the memories wanted to get in, and he knew he couldn't keep them out much longer and would have to host them one by one....

He lay staring at the ceiling.

12

Having slept little since getting the news, he finally dozed off, and when there was a knock on his door he was deeply befuddled as to where he was and what was going on.

"Kenny," his father's voice said.

He lay still, waiting for awareness to swim up to the surface.

He said, "Just a minute." He swiveled himself off the bed, dug at his eyes and forehead.

He opened the door.

"Got something for you," his father said. He was holding a grainy, light blue envelope toward him.

He took it, said "Thanks," and closed the door.

He went back to the bed, sat down on it, and looked at the envelope.

He saw his name written in a sloped, elegant, unfamiliar hand, followed by the address here in Willowcreek Park.

He looked at the top left corner and saw "Colleen Grady" and an address in Massachusetts.

He stared before him.

He reminded himself that he didn't know her last name; it was probably some other Colleen, not her.

He opened the envelope and pulled out some pages of light blue stationery.

He held the pages before him and read what was written in the same sloped hand:

April 7, 1974

Dear Kenny,

First of all, a minor confession: I called the operator in your area and was able to find out that you, or at least your family, are still at the same address. So I think—I hope—I can rest assured that you'll at least, one way or the other, receive this!

And I guess it will be a big surprise for you to get it! I, for my part, would not be surprised if you hate me now for taking three years to answer your letter, and won't even want to read what I'm sending you now. And I could understand that. But I hope, Kenny, that you'll at least want to hear what I have to say—it's important to me.

I'm writing—as you've seen if you've glanced at the return address—from Banford, which is a really cute little town up here in northern Massachusetts by the seashore, and the home of Banford College, where I'm in my sophomore year. I might even have mentioned it to you back in our Blue Spruce Lake days. As it turned out, while I applied to some other places too, I got a really good scholarship offer from Banford and that pretty much decided it. And— turns out—I don't regret it because it's really nice

here, and—surprise, surprise (it surprises me!)—
things are going quite well for me here.

Kenny, when I received your letter just about
three years ago I was very surprised and my initial reaction—I mean my instinctive, "normal" reaction—
was very positive; I had to put some effort into con-
vincing myself to keep being angry and rejecting toward you (and wasn't I all too good at that). About
my little brother, Billy, going up to your bungalow
at the end just before we left—yes, that did happen.
And yes, I had "sent" him. It was really at the last
minute and—as I see it now, as I can understand it
now—a ray of sanity broke through and suddenly I
realized that, if I didn't say something to you (and
yes, the thought of giving you my address was part
of it), it meant we were going our different ways for
good—really for good. And so I "sent" Billy to tell
you I wanted to talk to you. I was afraid to go to your
bungalow myself because I was sure you hated me
by then—which would have been quite understandable! And Billy resented what he saw as my bossing
him around—also quite understandable—and didn't
feel comfortable about the whole thing, and backed
off, and next thing I knew I was in our car and it
was pulling away and I was alone with my (as usual)
confused, crazy thoughts.

I have good friends here, but in particular I've
encountered two wonderful people who've really
gone a long way to (I think!) getting me unconfused
and (dare I say it??) uncrazed. One is my boyfriend,
Reg, a wonderful guy and a history major. And the
other is my therapist, Denise. You might remember

that back in those days I didn't go for any kind of therapy, because I refused to ask various people for money. Well, up here it turned out there was an almost-free service through the college, and pretty soon after starting here I decided to give it a try—and how thankful I am that at least—for once!—I made a good decision.

Kenny, this is a long story, but basically Denise and I have concentrated on—of course—the traumatic things that happened to me, and also on (after a few years I still feel comfortable talking to you about personal matters!) getting me not to view the world always from the standpoint of those traumatic things. Which includes not relating to people in anger when it's not called for, or at least not with a degree of anger that's not called for. That has to do with my mother and my stepfather. And it also has to do with you. Recently I've talked with Denise at length about the episode that we had, and I hope that doesn't disturb you in terms of respecting your privacy, but you can be 100% sure that everything remains between me and her. I was able to tell her because I still remember quite well what happened in those four (or three and a half!) days (still hard to believe that that's all it was). And of course—with her help—I arrived at the realization (as I've hinted, a part of me already knew it) that my anger and cruelty toward you were totally out of line and totally undeserved. And Kenny, that is one of the reasons I'm writing to you—because I want to make amends to people I've unfairly hurt and you are definitely one of them.

I understand now how cruel I was that morning by the dock, and also by leaving your letter unanswered. I've had lots of things to talk with Denise about—including how to deal with Reg—how to accept what he wants to give me and not reject it (unfortunately not simple in my case)—and it's more recently that we've been focusing on you and what happened between us at the lake that summer (quite a complicated subject in itself!). So this, in a roundabout way, is how I'm apologizing to you for taking so long to answer your letter (which was sweet!), and of saying—I'm sorry, and I hope you can forgive me. Of course, you may well have written me off a long, long time ago, which would be very understandable!

But as you see—bad as my behavior toward you has been—I have never written you off, never stopped thinking about those days, and I still hope that we can be "on good terms again" (as you put it in your letter) because, Kenny, I'm trying to put together again what has been a pretty disrupted life.

And now, finally—about you! It was just about exactly three years ago that you were nice enough to tell me (in your letter) about your basketball success (being on the varsity team!), the end of your "official" career, and your starting to read books again. So by now—if I can guess—I'd guess that you're in one of our higher education institutions and doing a lot more reading! But anyway, Kenny, instead of me guessing—I would love to hear from you. To tell me any reactions you might have to this letter, and to tell me how you're doing!

Thanks for bearing with me for this long—if you have!

Please write!!
Your friend,
Colleen

Having sat there almost trancelike, he finally lowered the letter, set it beside him on the bed.

He got up and walked to the window, the one that looked out on the side yard.

The spring day was bright and placid, as if everything had always been the same.

Motionless, seeing but not really seeing, he said, "I told you she'd answer. *I told you she'd answer.*"

13

When they got back from the funeral it was the dusk hour; the sky was deep grey, there were a few stars in it, a few birds sang with a sweet languidness, the lilac scent hung heavy. They all—elegantly dressed—went into the house without a word. He went to his room, closed the door, and lay on his bed. He heard Lizzie, next door, doing things—but unlike every other evening of her life at this hour, not calling a friend on the phone.

The dark grew and he heard, distant and jubilant, the spring peepers.

He got up, turned on the light, went out to the small foyer where the phone sat on its table.

He took it into his room, closed the door on the cord. The cord wasn't long, and when he sat on his bed to talk on the phone, he had to sit perched uncomfortably at the edge of it.

Sitting there, he looked again at the envelope that was lying on the bed, read the return address again.

He called two operators. He asked the second one for the phone number of Colleen Grady at 38 Devonshire Street. It seemed she was living somewhere in the town, not in a dorm.

The operator started giving him the number; he said, "One minute, please." He took a pen and notepad from his desk, went back and picked up the receiver again with his left hand, said, "What was that, please?"

He dialed the number. As he heard the ring—once, twice, thrice—he told himself it still wasn't too late, he could still hang up.

He heard the phone get picked up in the middle of the fourth ring.

"Hello?"

"Hello," he said.

"Hello?"

"Hello. Is this Colleen?"

"No, this is her roommate. Just a minute, I'll get her."

He heard muffled voices; then, after a few seconds: "Hello?"

"Hello?"

"Hello."

"Hello, Colleen?"

"Yes, this is Colleen."

"Hi. It's Kenny."

"*Kenny.*"

"Yeah…hope it's OK that I'm calling."

"*Kenny*…! I thought it was you! So you got my letter!"

"Yes. I got it today. Thanks. I got your number from the operator. I really wanted to talk to you. I hope it's OK."

"Of course it's OK. Are you all right?"

"Not really."

"I didn't think so, you sound…did my letter upset you? I'm sorry."

"Colleen. Your letter didn't upset me at all."

"Oh. It didn't? That's good. But…where are you?"

"I'm home. At my parents' house."

"Oh… Oh. Did something happen?"

"Yeah, you could say that."

"Kenny. What happened?"

"Well, I don't know if you remember, if I ever told you back then, about my friend Leon."

"Your friend Leon. Yes. Of course. He was your best friend, right?"

"Right. Was."

"Was? *Was.* Kenny. What happened?"

"Well, he died a couple of days ago in a car accident."

"Oh my God."

"I was at Binghamton, that's where I go to school. My parents called to tell me. So I had to come home today for the funeral. I was just at the funeral."

"Oh Kenny. I'm...I'm shocked."

"I got here today in the morning, and a little after that, my father comes to my door and says, 'Got something for you,' and he gives me your letter. It's...it's all pretty crazy."

"Kenny, it's...I can't believe it. I so wanted that to be a happy moment for you. I *hoped*.... Oh, God."

"Colleen, I feel like I need to talk to you."

"Sure...sure. My boyfriend's coming in about fifteen minutes to pick me up, that's the thing. We had something planned tonight. I'm sorry. I'm really sorry. Tomorrow would be fine. Would that be OK? Or...we can wait to go out. So you and I can talk. It's fine."

"Colleen, no need to wait. I was just thinking...would I be able to come out there so we can talk?"

"To come out here? To Banford?"

"Yeah."

"Yes... Yes. That would be fine. When would you want to come?"

"Well, tomorrow I have to go to this thing with friends of Leon, who are mostly friends of mine. We were all pretty much the same crowd. But I thought, maybe, if I could come on the weekend."

"The weekend. Kenny, I'm really sorry. Reg and I—that's my boyfriend—we have things planned for this weekend. I'm really sorry. Would Monday work out for you?"

"Monday, let's see. Yeah, that would be fine. If we could meet, say, in the afternoon. Then I could get back home, take the bus back to Binghamton Tuesday morning. Can miss one more day of classes, doesn't matter."

"OK. We could meet, like—at a café on campus. Would that be OK?"

"Yeah, fine."

"OK. I'll have to tell you how to get there. You'll be coming by car?"

"Yeah, I think so. Think my parents will give me the Pontiac for it."

"OK. Great. Kenny we can talk meanwhile. I can't now, but tomorrow?"

"That's all right, Colleen. Like I said, I've got this thing tomorrow, then you've got things on the weekend. After so much time, I'd really rather we talk in person anyway. I think it's just nicer that way."

"Oh. All right. Yeah, that should be nice. But Kenny. Are you OK?"

"I'm all right, Colleen. I'm OK. We'll talk more about it on Monday."

"I'm so sorry…. This is such a terrible thing."

"It's all right, Colleen."

"Let me just…let me just ask my roommate about the directions, she'll know them better than I do. A minute, OK?"

14

When he saw her his heart turned over. She was more filled out; her black hair was shorter, surrounding her face in two thick, glossy concavities that curved outward at her neck. But her eyes had the same look they'd sometimes had, back then, when she was calm—only more so; something at once alert, patient, and affable.

She was waiting at the appointed time, two o'clock, by the café, which was on a little plateau at the northern edge of the campus, which was small enough that almost all of it could be seen from the plateau. The café was a squat affair with brick walls and a sign over the entrance saying, in red calligraphy, The Hideaway. Behind it the plateau fell away to a stretch of tawny, rocky beach, fronting the sea.

It was a bright, cool April day, and she wore a light blue windbreaker over a pink top, tied with lace at the throat, and jeans. She came toward him as if on a gust, and they hugged. He closed his eyes and hugged her a little madly, already beyond the limit he thought he'd set for himself.

"Colleen," he said with a smile, "this is weird."

"I know."

"I didn't think I'd see you again. It's almost surreal."

"Kenny I know just what you mean."

She was sitting across from him, her back to where people took food at the serving counter. He'd taken almost his only food, so far, of the day—a Western egg sandwich, French fries, and coffee. She, saying she'd already eaten, had taken just a coffee and cake. The café was a single, spacious room with wood paneling and tables for four; a picture window to his right showed the sky and, at a distance, the sea.

The jacket now hung behind her on her chair; he could see her in just the very short-sleeved pink top.

She said, "How you feeling?"

"Not wonderful. I don't know, it's mixed up. It's crazy."

He said, "Berkshires were beautiful. I didn't want to see them that much, though. After what happened...I don't know. Didn't want to see everything coming to life."

"Kenny. I can understand that."

She said, "When Scott got killed it was March. Seeing everything come to life again...that was hell."

He said, "You wouldn't believe this, but..."

He stopped; he gazed out toward the right, as if seeking some answer from the view.

He said, "A very short time after my parents called me in my dorm room...to tell me what happened...I talked to you in my mind."

She said, "What did you say?"

"I just said...how much I wished I could talk to you at that moment."

She gazed at a spot on the table.

She said, "Did you do that very much?"

"What. Talk to you in my mind?"

"Yeah."

"Yeah. As time went on I did it less. But still from time to time."

They both fell silent.

She said, finally, "You and Leon went back a long way, right?"

"Fifth grade. Best friends, unbelievably close."

"Where was he when this happened?"

"Ithaca, in western New York. He was going to school at Cornell. He was a physics major there. Leon was really bright. But he had a wild streak. When it happened, in Ithaca, he was driving a car that his parents bought him, after leaving a bar."

She dropped her forehead into her hands. She sat like that for some time.

She drew her hands away, and her face looked haggard.

She said, "Kenny. I have a lot I want to ask you. But maybe it's not the right time."

"Colleen...whatever you want to ask, you should ask it."

She gave him a stationary, bright gaze, as if trying to decide if she believed him.

She said, "Kenny, when you wrote me that letter three years ago...what was going on?"

"Actually it was...it was another one of these things with spring. I couldn't really get over what happened in those days at the lake. Actually, there were sort of phases...phases where I really thought about it a lot, and then there were phases where I seemed to have stopped, or almost stopped. I think what kept bringing me back was that thing about your brother—my sister telling me that at the very end there, he almost came up to our house. I couldn't just—I couldn't just set aside the idea that maybe you still wanted to say something to me. And then it was spring and—everything was moving forward, and that really depressed me, because I felt like I was, you know, supposed to move forward with it, but that would mean—turning my back on what happened, saying goodbye to it, and I couldn't do that. So finally my father asked me what was getting me down so much, and I told him the whole story. And then he said he could get your address, or your family's address, pretty easily…and he did. And I wrote to you."

"And what happened"—she said it glumly—"when I didn't answer?"

"Ohh…Leon tried to set me up with someone else. Pretty nice girl actually. But she lived kind of far away, and also…she saw that I was still pretty hung up on you."

"You were still hung up on me when I didn't write?"

"Yeah."

"Kenny. But you've been…you've been involved with girls."

"Yes. A couple while I was still in school, a couple at Binghamton. But nothing much comes of it."

"Why does nothing much come of it?"

"I don't know, maybe not the right girls…. Or maybe because nothing meets the gold standard."

"And what…is the gold standard."

"It's, uh…those days by the lake. Even if they were complicated. Even if they didn't end wonderfully."

She viewed him with a kind of bleak intensity.

"Wasn't there something with Israel? Weren't you supposed to go to Israel that summer?"

"Oh, that." He smiled. "That was nice. I was at a kibbutz in the Galilee. For two weeks. I picked grapes. Worked with the chickens, too. And the cows."

She gave him a bright, complex, stationary look.

"That was *nice*?"

He smiled. "Not so much the work. The place. It's beautiful up there. Also the people. There were other volunteers, from all over the place, but I got to hang around with the Israeli kids, too. They're really different. They're cynical on the outside—the guys, not so much the girls—but there's more of a collective thing there. The country's still a big thing for everyone. I don't know, you have to experience it. I feel like I'd like to go back there one way or another."

He looked at her.

He said, with a small smile, "Yes, there was a girl. Orly. We were supposed to keep in touch, but her English wasn't that good. I still have a couple of her letters somewhere, where she tries to write English. It's cute."

She said, "So. Binghamton?"

"Yeah. I was surprised I got in, actually, because my grades weren't that good. I kind of slacked off in high school. But... English major. I really like it. Reading books all the time like I did as a kid. Except that now I also have to write about them. Write papers. But...I've actually gotten to like that, too."

"Great."

She said, "Like father like son."

"Yeah. Except he's more of a writer. He's a writer through and through. I'm more of a reader. I mean, I have to read something before I can write anything. Write about what I've read."

He encircled his cup with his fingers, jiggled the tiny amount of coffee still left in it.

"I'm going to get another of these, and some kind of dessert. You want something else?"

"Just another coffee. Thanks, Kenny."

15

When he came back to the table with their things on a tray, she looked almost as if she hadn't moved; sitting, a little back from the table and turned a little to the left, with a distant, contemplative expression.

He sank back into his chair, putting the tray on the table. Her eyes moved to the tray as if it were some sort of discovery for her.

He said, "Brought sugar for you because I don't know how much you take."

"Thanks Kenny." She started assembling her coffee, still with a distracted air.

He said, "You do seem different."

She moved her eyes slowly to his.

"*I* seem different?"

"Yeah."

"How so?"

"Less angry."

She stirred her coffee, lifted it for a sip, set it down.

"I'm still angry Kenny."

She said, "But I'm trying to do something with it."

"What are you doing with it?"

"Well...I decided to be a psych major."

She said, "What I want to do…I want to work with people who went through the kind of thing I went through with the creep. That way…I don't know. Maybe something good can come of it."

"That sounds great, Colleen."

He said, "Did Denise—that's her name, right?—did she help you decide that?"

"Yeah… For a while we were talking about taking the legal tack. My mother knows where he is now. In Michigan. But—" she raised her hands and dropped them on the table. "So many years later. Without any kind of proof."

"So your mother knows about it now."

"Yes."

"Back then…I remember you told me you wouldn't tell her about it."

"Right. I wouldn't."

She said, "Kenny this is hard to talk about."

"We don't have to. It's OK."

"No I want to."

She said, "Want you to know, Kenny."

She sighed deeply.

"I told Denise about how—when it was going on—I kept it from her. From my mother. How I thought she wouldn't believe me. She said that probably wasn't true. She said I needed to tell her. So. It was still very tough for me so I agreed that we'd invite her to come—from New Jersey—to one of our meetings. With me and Denise. And she did."

She leaned forward with her hands pressing the sides of her face.

"This is the hard part Kenny."

She said, "So. I told her that it happened. That it was him who did it. And…she just about collapsed."

He reached out and put his hand on her forearm.

She said, "Don't do that Kenny OK?"

He moved his hand away.

She said, "I haven't seen any friends of Reg here, but… who knows."

She said, "The main thing is…it was real. Totally real. She was horrified beyond belief."

She slowly unwound, sat back in her chair.

He said, "I noticed back then—she was always worried about you. I know she was a pain in the ass about it—get home in time for supper and all that. But I noticed that she seemed to care about you at least."

"She is not my favorite person Kenny. Not when she started bringing men home and having loud sex with them right after my father took off. Not when she kept doing it for years. Not when she sent me to help that creep with cooking his meals. But…" Again—more heavily—she dropped her hands on the table. "I guess the point is that she wasn't the monster I made her out to be."

She said, "Kenny, when you met me I was a coiled spring."

"Well. I won't argue with that."

He said, "So do you get along with her now?"

"A little better. It's never going to be the world's greatest friendship. But. Yeah. A little better."

He said, "What about your stepfather."

"Oh, that."

She said, "I probably told you he was ogling me all the time, right?"

"You wouldn't even go down to the beach to swim."

"Right… So, I went into that with Denise, too. I described everything to her. He wasn't really doing it that much. He tried to control it. I was…well you know how I was. All men are monsters, blah blah."

"Yup."

"I'm actually—now—kind of friendly with him. More so than with my mother. Ron's not my favorite person either. He's…you know. A lowlife. Like my mother. But actually, if I had to choose between the two of them, I'd take him. He's a bit more normal."

"I noticed, back then, that he seemed to get along with your brother.'

"Yes. He's quite nice to Billy. Almost"—she moved her hand on the table—"a father to him."

Neither of them spoke.

He said, "Well Colleen. I'm glad that you're not surrounded by monsters after all."

She moved her eyes to his.

"No. They might start to seem more monstrous again if I had to be around them a lot. But…I don't have to anymore."

He looked out the window at the view.

"Colleen, would you want to go down there and sit by the water? For old times' sake."

She, too, looked at the view, as if to make sure it was all there.

"Kenny. Reg is very jealous."

"Of us?"

"In general. If he saw us down there…really bad."

"He knows we're here, right?"

"Yes. Of course. In a café. But if he saw us down there… Or if someone he knows saw us down there, and told him…"

He gazed off at the view.

"I came all the way out here, and you're going to deny me a walk by the ocean?"

The sea was a muted turquoise color, the sky an innocent April blue as if the world were getting a new chance. They sat in the sand not far from the water. Though the sun was behind them, sinking westward, it was still warm in its light. He took off his jacket, tossed it beside him.

He said, "So Leon's gone."

He picked up a pebble beside him, tossed it into the water. It plopped a couple of yards into the slow-moving, dull turquoise tide.

She said, "I don't think he's gone."

He looked at her.

"No?"

"No. I never believed that about Scott."

"Why not?"

"Because I don't believe that someone like him just disappears."

"So what does that mean? He's somewhere else?"

"I think so."

"What about Leon?"

"Kenny. I talked about Scott because I knew him. Of course, Leon too."

"So I don't have to feel horrible?"

"I didn't say that, Kenny. *We* lose them. We don't have them in our lives anymore. In these lives. That's horrible enough."

"And what about them. What about the things they could have been, and can never be now."

"That's an awful thing too."

"But they're not gone totally."

"No."

"You're Catholic, right?"

"Yeah. How did you know?"

"Grady's an Irish name. Usually Catholic."

He said, "You go to church?"

"You might not believe it, but my mother—of all people—would take us to church sometimes when we were little."

"You go now?"

"Now? No. Not really."

She said, "But what I think isn't dependent on that."

"No?"

"No. I just think what makes sense to me."

"So what makes sense to you? The soul lives on?"

"Yes."

She said, "You religious at all?"

"Me? Nah. I told you, I think, my father's Jewish. My mother's Methodist. But both of them are totally unreligious. I've got—no religious background to speak of."

He said, "And I think—if there was a God—and he was so great—that things like this, a young person getting killed for no reason, wouldn't happen."

"Well Kenny, there might be reasons for things that we don't understand. We're just little people."

"Well. I guess."

He picked up another pebble, tossed it into the water.

Squinting into the distance, he said, "Is that an island out there?"

"Yes. It's Hulett Island."

"Yeah? Here's our chance."

She looked at him.

She said, "I think there's a guy renting out a rowboat just down the beach here."

"Rowboat shmowboat. Let's swim there."

"Kenny what a wonderful idea."

She said, "Reg and I have been out there."

"Yeah?"

"Yeah, in a boat. A real boat. It's really great. Saw whales out there."

"Yeah?"

"You know what, it's hot here."

She shrugged out of her jacket and laid it beside her; he saw the down on her sunlit bare arm.

Shielding her eyes from the sun, she peered down the beach to right and left; then wheeled her body to gaze upward at the café on its hill.

"Anyone watching us?"

"Not down here, at least." She returned to facing forward, but sullenly. "From up there…who knows."

"So he's a jealous type?"

"Reg?"

"Yeah."

"Yes, he is."

"He make trouble for you?"

She looked at him.

"You don't have to worry about this, Kenny."

"Well. I want to know about it. That OK?"

"I guess so."

"So," he said.

"So what?"

"So, he makes trouble?"

"Yeah, I guess you could say that."

"What kind of trouble?"

"I don't know…. I have a teacher for Psych 200, Ed Bentley. Young guy, maybe thirty-five. Real good-looking. Girls are all nuts about him. You go for a tutorial with him once a week. When I go…Reg gets all paranoid."

"He have a reason to?"

"No. Kenny I'm really not like that. Yeah he's good-looking. But I don't think of him that way."

"But Reg gets paranoid?"

"Yeah."

"What does he do? Shove you around?"

"Kenny for God's sake. You think I'd stay with him if he did that?"

She said, "He just starts throwing out these little accusations. It's basically pathetic. They're really…pleas. Pleas to be reassured."

"So you reassure him?"

"Yeah. What do you think I do?"

"So he knows about this meeting of ours?"

"Of course he does. I told you he does."

"He OK with it?"

"OK with it…? No. Not really."

"He knows the story?"

"What. The lake?"

"Yeah."

"Yes."

"The *whole* story?"

"The whole story."

She said, "I had to talk with Denise about it. She said to emphasize that you'd lost a friend, that you were depressed."

"So that got him to agree to it?"

"I guess so."

"He wouldn't have agreed to it otherwise?"

"I'm not sure. Maybe not."

"Well. You could have just told me to forget it."

She looked at him.

"I didn't want to do that."

"No?"

"No."

"Why not?"

"Because I wanted to meet with you."

"Why. Because you felt sorry for me?"

"No. Not because I felt sorry for you. Because I wanted to meet with you."

"Oh."

He sat forward, dusted the sand off his hands, settled back with his elbows in the sand again.

He said, "It's not comfortable sitting like this."

"Well who insisted on going down here."

"Me."

"Want me to bring a blanket?"

"Sure."

"You'd like that, wouldn't you."

"Yeah, sure."

He said, "So what else does he do."

She turned halfway toward him.

"What do you mean, what else does he do."

"I assume that his jealousy is not directed solely at this handsome teacher."

"Oh. No. Not solely at that person. What can I say, Kenny. I go places in the world, and there are guys in the world. Sometimes I talk with them. Sometimes I meet with them. It's hard for him. He has a hard time with it."

"This is something that you need?"

She turned and looked briefly at him, as if surveying him.

She said, "These girls that you've been with…were they perfect?"

"No. But I didn't stay with them."

"Well, you want me to start listing for you all of Reg's great traits? You probably don't want that."

"Nah. That does sound a little boring, to tell you the truth."

"Yeah, I thought so."

They both fell quiet for a time. The tide moved in leisurely over the sand, then flowed back leaving the sand dark and glossy.

He said, "It's like those days a few years ago but it's not like them. I don't know. It's hard to put into words."

"Kenny I know what you mean."

He sat gazing at the water running up and down the glossy sand.

He put a finger on her forearm and began moving it gently along the skin.

"Kenny."

"What."

"What are you doing?"

"What do you think I'm doing?"

"Well you can't do it."

He held his finger still.

"Colleen. It's in the shade. See? Our bodies are making shade. Even if someone's really peering at us from the window of the café, even if they have X-ray vision, they can't see it."

He moved his finger up further, stroked the soft flesh in the crook of her arm.

"Kenny *stop*. Really."

He moved his hand away.

He said, "Colleen. You're nineteen years old. You're not married to Reg."

"Correct. Correct. I just happen to love him."

"Even with the trouble he makes for you?"

She said, "What. You're with someone, you're never jealous?"

"Only if there's a reason for it. I'm not neurotic about it."

"Nobody's perfect, are they, Kenny?"

"Suppose not."

"See, this is what I talked with Denise about."

"What. What did you talk with her about?"

"That I wanted to meet with you, and I wanted it to be nice. I didn't want it to be something where I'm hurting you again."

"And what did she say?"

"She said you'd probably moved on and it would be all right."

"Well. Maybe she was wrong about me moving on."

He said, "How do you see yourself as having hurt me in the first place?"

She gave him a dully uncertain look.

He said, "Aside from taking three years to answer my letter. How do you see yourself as hurting me back then?"

She took out a moment or two for dull uncertainty.

"Bawling you out that morning by the dock? Telling you to get lost? That was really cruel. Wasn't it?"

"Yeah. But you had a reason for it."

He said, "You said I pressured you into doing something you didn't want to do."

"Right. Which was totally untrue."

He looked at her.

"Now you think it was untrue?"

She said, "Kenny. What happened that night by the lake happened because I wanted it to happen. You didn't make me do anything. Yeah, I had inner conflict. One side of the inner conflict won out. Even if it didn't totally win out. That's why it happened. I was pushing for it too. I knew we didn't have much time. I didn't want to leave there without that having happened. I just couldn't be honest with myself about it."

"Why not?"

"Because I was mad at myself."

She said, "I couldn't accept the whole thing. It wasn't just the problem I had with guys. With men. Whatever. It was also… I told you about my mother. How she'd get it on with guys in my earshot starting when I was a little kid. So I had associations. Associations with sex. And they were really bad. Couldn't accept myself in that role."

She sat with both arms hugging one knee, looking down at the sand.

"So. I took it all out on you. Convinced myself that it happened because you forced it to happen. Which was totally wrong. Not least because you're not someone who would ever force something like that to happen."

He said, "So what are we going to do with me now."

She looked at him as if trying hard to see him.

"What are we going to do with you?"

"Seems like I haven't moved on."

He said, "I feel a bond with you Colleen. Haven't felt it with anyone else. I guess I'll have to keep looking. I'll probably find something."

She said, "Why do you think it is?"

"What. The bond?"

"Yeah."

"I don't know…. You're deep. Deep and intense."

He said, "And you want to do good. Always. Even when you're a coiled spring, you have to convince yourself that what you're doing is good. It's…it's pretty charming."

He said, "Or maybe something just happened to me at the island."

144

She said, after a while, "Well, you should not feel that you're alone in this."

"No?"

"No. I feel the bond too. It's two-way. But…time went on and I met Reg. He's a great guy too."

He said, "Yup."

He said, "So where does this leave us?"

She said, "It leaves me hoping we can have a nice connection without anyone being hurt."

"How. How do we have this connection?"

"Well. There's a Reg problem…. Not that he exists but the way he is."

She said, "We write letters from time to time. Not too often, unfortunately. And from time to time…we meet. In a café in the afternoon or something like that. Not sitting together by the sea."

He picked up a pebble, tossed it into the tide.

He said, "'The question that he frames in all but words / Is what to make of a diminished thing.'"

"What's that?"

"It's from a poem. By Robert Frost."

"It's nice."

She said, "Well, even if it's diminished. *If* it's diminished. That's better than losing it. Isn't it?'

"Yeah. I think so."

PART FOUR: MAY 1980

16

Ken told the hostess that "There'll be two of us." Asked where they'd be wanting to sit, he said, "Outside." He said he'd meanwhile wait in the lobby for "my friend."

It was one of Binghamton's nicer restaurants. Having had two dates with Rochelle, it had seemed to him that things were moving in a certain direction, and that the time was right to ask her out to such a place. She'd answered with a clear yes.

He'd seen her around for some time. They were in related fields; he was now going for his doctorate in English, she for hers in comp lit. But it was only a few weeks ago, at a retirement party for a professor they both knew, that he'd found himself talking with her. It kept going and going, as if they'd been storing up things to say to each other.

It was now a warm night in late May, and he was glad of the chance to stand here in the air-conditioning, feeling the sweat dry. In the dim light, a group of other waiters-for-a-seat were sitting on a long couch along the wall. From inside came sounds of a solo electric-guitar album by Joe Pass. It was one of the town's only restaurants that played more subdued, cerebral music.

The door opened, and Rochelle came in. He saw that she was honoring the occasion: hoop earrings, a several-strand pearl necklace, a short, maroon dress fit for a prom. When she saw him she brightened subtly, as if they shyly shared a secret.

"Hi."

"Hi."

"Wait long?"

"Nah. I said we wanted to sit outside. That OK?"

"Outside" meant a spacious flagstone veranda between the restaurant and, behind a stone wall, a side street. The hostess sat them at a small round table beside the wall of the restaurant; right above them a speaker piped the guitar music. The other tables were moderately populated. The night was now consenting to let breezes blow. He looked up at the stars.

He said, "Nice."

"Yes."

She sat—characteristically—very still, her eyes fixed on him.

Rochelle had bright, very straight blond hair, combed back from her forehead; very clear, alert eyes of an usual silvery-green hue; something of the dignified reserve of a Medici queen. He knew that she was from Long Island; had—like him—a Jewish father and a Protestant mother; had been an undergrad at Carnegie Mellon, then a grad student at Binghamton; was a year older than him and further along in her doctorate-writing.

"Well," he said. "Looks like I've got good work—relatively good—for the summer."

"Yeah?"

"My father talked with a guy at his publisher, and it looks like they're willing to send me books. For appraisals. Whether they should publish them, or what changes the author should make before they can publish them. These would be books they're already interested in, not just, you know, from what they call the slush pile."

"That sounds good."

"It does. Beats working in a supermarket."

She smiled. "That's what you did last summer?"

"Not last summer, but a few of the summers I was here, yes, it's what I did."

"I came across your father's books in the library. Wow. There are a lot of them."

"He's published something like twenty-five by now. Been churning them out since as long as I can remember."

"So productive."

"Yes. And his life—on the outside, at least—is pretty ordinary. I asked him once where he gets all the ideas. He said, pretty much, that he just puts pen to paper and trusts that something will emerge. And it does."

"Hm. These people like…Trollope…or Balzac. They could just churn them out. Seems like the energy is endless."

"Yes. My father seems to have something of that. He'd be happy if he could have the fame of Trollope or Balzac, though. Or even one-tenth of it."

A waitress came up to them, bearing menus, and asked if meanwhile they would want something to drink. He asked for a gin and tonic, she for a daiquiri. The waitress set the thick menus on the table.

"Talk about books," he said, picking up his menu and leafing through it.

"What?"

"This menu is like a book."

"Oh. Right. Almost like one of those Thomas Wolfe books you read."

They read their menus and sipped their drinks, not saying much. When the waitress returned with a pen and a pad, Rochelle ordered a meal centering on salmon, and Ken—a vegetarian—a meal centering on a baked potato stuffed with broccoli.

The waitress swept up the menus, asked them if they wanted more to drink, and when they both said they were fine, walked off with an air of satisfied efficiency.

She said, "You met with Michaelson?"

"Yes," he said. "Yes. It went well. Really well."

"Great."

"He's a Wolfe holdout like me. I'm glad there's at least one Wolfe loyalist on the faculty."

"You really like Wolfe."

"Yes. I think he was a really wonderful writer. I know it's a dissenting opinion now. Got some faults, yes. But who doesn't."

"So what did Michaelson say?"

"Well, he's quite happy with the idea I came up with for the thesis. 'Mourning as Catalyst in the Fiction of Thomas Wolfe.'"

"Mourning...as catalyst. Mourning with a *u*?"

"Right. The idea is that when Wolfe constantly reverts to mourning, he's sort of recharging the batteries. He can't get into the other stuff—the nature ecstasies and so on—unless the mourning is in place. Something like that."

"Sounds like that mourning really speaks to you."

"Hm. Yeah. I guess it does."

"Why do you think that is?"

"Hm." He held his glass as it stood on the table.

"Well"—lifting his gaze to hers—"I told you about my friend Leon."

"Yes."

"That's a large part of my past, unfortunately. The memories are there—but they're all under that shadow."

"Yes. I can imagine what that must be like."

She said, "You seem kind of down."

"I seem down?"

"Sort of."

"Hm. Yeah. I got a letter today. Maybe that has something to do with it. I wouldn't say down. Worried maybe."

"A letter."

"Yeah."

"Who…was the author of this letter?"

"The author was…Colleen. I told you about her, right?"

"A little."

"Yeah. Well… There are problems with her husband. It's kind of…I don't know."

She took a sip of her drink, sat back in her chair, folded her arms on her stomach, gazed at him.

"Yeah. You told me she was married."

"Right."

"Maybe you should tell me more."

"About Colleen?"

"Mm-hm."

"Well. What would you like to know about her?"

"You've known her a while?"

"Yeah. Since we were both sixteen. Both of our families happened to be at the same vacation place on Blue Spruce Lake. Know Blue Spruce Lake?"

"Yes, of course. In the Adirondacks."

"Right… Well. We had a brief, tempestuous romance there."

"Tem*pes*tuous."

She gave him a very subtle smile.

"What could have made it tem*pes*tuous? Sounds like it should have been idyllic. On a mountain lake."

"Yeah. Should have been… I guess she was in a more tempestuous state than I was to begin with."

"*She* was."

"Yeah."

"Why was that?"

"Well…she wasn't in good shape. She was from a difficult background. Including abuse by a boyfriend of her mother."

"Oh, dear."

"Yeah, so…she couldn't handle having a romance. She kind of tore it down after it started."

The waitress came with their food on a cart. He wasn't comfortable; he knew that, once the waitress had finished doling out the food, he'd have to keep telling her the story because she was on the trail of something now. He wished he hadn't mentioned Colleen's letter. He could have said he was "down" for some other reason, or just denied it.

They each ordered a second drink, and Rochelle also asked for ice water.

She looked down at her food, which was very generously supplied.

"Well. That does look inviting."

She started to pick at the food delicately with a fork.

"Hmm…this salmon."

"What?"

"Not sure. Could be better. Maybe."

The waitress came back with their second round of drinks; they sat silently and dutifully as she set them before them.

"So," she said after the waitress melted away again. "This thing seems to have continued somehow. After the tempest."

"Yeah… What happened was, about half a year later, I wrote her a letter. To New Jersey. She lived in New Jersey. And…after three years she answered."

"Three years."

"Yup."

"Sounds like she wasn't in a great rush."

"No, definitely not. By that time she was at Banford College in Massachusetts, and, uh…she was in intensive therapy. She was getting over her anger at various people. I was on the list, and she wanted to come clean with me, and she finally wrote me a letter. The strange thing was that it arrived on the day of Leon's funeral. He'd gotten killed two days earlier, and I'd just come home from Binghamton, for the funeral, and I was in my room, not in a wonderful state as you can imagine, and my father comes and knocks on my door and says 'Got something for you.' It was her letter."

"Wow. That must have been an insane day for you."

"Yes. Very insane. The letter said she was sorry, she was sorry for the tempest and for not answering my letter for so long. She did make clear that she had a boyfriend. So… that night, after the funeral, feeling quite horrible as you can imagine, I called her, and a few days later I went out there and met with her. Just sat with her in the afternoon. And since then we've been in touch again."

She regarded him with her silver-green gaze.

"And what does 'in touch' mean?"

"Means we write letters, and also we get together once in a while. We get together where she lives, not where I live. The boyfriend—the husband—is quite the jealous type. He couldn't stand for her coming to visit me."

"Wait—the boyfriend—the husband—it's the same person?"

"Right. The same guy she was already with at Banford. They're married a couple of years now."

The guitar music had stopped, and now the speaker above them piped the first hummed, thrummed notes of "The Girl from Ipanema" on the *Getz/Gilberto* album.

"Oh, I love this," he said.

"It's samba, right?"

"Bossa nova. Related to samba."

"But it's jazz, right?"

"Yes. It's sort of a fusion of the two."

"You're quite into jazz."

"Yes. Yes, I am."

The waitress materialized again and said, "Everything OK?"

"Actually," Rochelle said, "the salmon's a bit overcooked."

"Oh. I'm sorry. Would you want me to ask the chef to prepare you another?"

"No, that's OK. But...*maybe* you could mention to him that he could have gone a little easier on it."

"OK. Fine. I'll let him know. Everything else OK?"

"Um...yes."

"Sure," Ken said.

Rochelle gazed at him as the waitress faded off again.

"So. What's Colleen up to now?"

"A lot, actually. They've got a kid, by the way, a one-year-old boy. They live in Springfield and Colleen—for now—works part-time with a clinic that helps abuse victims. She was so impressed with the shrink she had at Banford that she majored in psych. And now she's doing...pretty much what she set out to do. Work with people who went through the kind of thing she went through."

"Hm."

She said, "Sounds like she's doing well."

"Yeah. She is."

"So…" she took a sip of her drink; set it back on the table, looked at him, her face a little flushed now from the drinking.

"So," she said. "Then what was this letter of hers today that kind of got you down?"

"Oh, that."

He sat back; he took a sip of his drink. Stan Getz's majestic sax solo on "Para Machucar Meu Coração" was playing now; the beauty made his insides curl up, but he couldn't say anything about it.

"Well," he said.

17

The other tables were more populated by now, the night darker and cooler, the stars brilliant. The voices, the clinks of dishes, and the music made for a soft elation.

He said, "This jealousy thing that Reg—the husband—has is quite a problem, and it's only getting worse.... Colleen has three half-siblings in Colorado. Her father...he pretty much abandoned them—I mean Colleen's side of the family, Colleen and her mother and her siblings—when Colleen was three. There's more to it than that, but... Anyway, among the many things that have weighed on Colleen was that she had almost no contact with these half-siblings, let alone her father. And so..."

He paused, sipped his drink.

"And so just lately one of the half-siblings—the oldest one, Justin—finally contacted Colleen. Turned out he needed to go to New York City for a couple of days—wants to check out Columbia as a possible grad school. He asked Colleen if, on the second day he's there, she could meet him in a restaurant in the afternoon. She was very thrilled by this because she really, really feels the absence of these people." His fingers closed around his glass and jostled it a little. "Unfortunately Reg feels differently about it. So...that was what the letter was about, for the most part."

"Her husband is objecting to that?"

"Right."

"This is her brother."

"Right."

Rochelle lifted up her glass very gently, held it to her lips, and sipped; she stared off toward the distance as if pondering very deeply.

"Sounds like this guy is quite a problem."

"He is."

"So…where does this stand now?"

He raised his hands and dropped them.

"Don't know. He's coming to New York in early June. As of three days ago it was unresolved."

He said, "She's tried to get the husband to go to a shrink for his problem, but she gave up a couple of years ago. He's got kind of a self-reliance ethos. He's from a rural part of Ontario, which could have something to do with it."

"Self-reliance as long as he's making problems for someone else."

"There's truth to that, unfortunately."

"So this is what's getting you down?"

"Yeah, it's…it's like an old blues song—'When things go wrong, so wrong with you, it hurts me too.'"

"When things go wrong with Colleen it hurts you too?"

"Yes, you could say that."

"So it sounds like you're pretty close."

"Yes. Yes. You could say that."

Rochelle—even though her eyelids were heavy and her cheeks flushed from the alcohol—had become very still again, looking at him levelly.

"So, do you think this is going to hold water between them?"

"The marriage?"

"Yeah."

"Yeah. I think it will, because Colleen's very idealistic about marriage. There are a lot of good things about Reg. He really loves the kid, too."

"But making trouble because she goes to see her brother?"

"Yeah. It's difficult."

"What do you think would happen if they did break up?"

He looked into her eyes with a small smile.

They sat looking wordlessly into each other's eyes, for the first time that night.

Above them, from the speaker, Astrud Gilberto sang, "Quiet nights of quiet stars, quiet chords from my guitar / Floating on the silence that surrounds us…"

She said, "I like being with you, Ken."

"Oh, thanks. I like being with you, too."

"But…*but*…I like to feel that the coast is clear."

"The coast is clear, Rochelle."

"Why?"

"Because they're not going to break up."

"But I want to know even theoretically—and I'm not convinced of that, by the way—what would happen if they did break up."

"If they did break up. Nothing would happen because I don't know if Colleen and I are a number anymore. And because I can't become a father to another man's kid, another man who would still be involved with the kid. Can't do that."

She seemed slowly and softly to process the words.

"But…"

"But…what?"

"That's not it."

"That's not it?"

"No."

"So what's it?"

"*It* is…not what would happen if this or that happened. It's…how you feel. About Colleen."

"How I feel about her."

"Right."

He said, "An argument of insidious intent…that leads to an overwhelming question. Something like that. I don't think that's exact."

He said, "How I feel about Colleen. She's one of the big people in my life. It's a deep friendship. Deep, mutually supportive friendship."

"That sounds nice."

"Yes, it is."

"What about…the tempest."

"The tempest."

He said, "Rochelle, I've had a little to drink, and also I have a habit of being honest. To a fault, maybe. OK, I will not say that the tempest has totally vanished from the earth. But. It's not something you would need to be concerned about."

"Why…is it not something that I would need to be concerned about?"

"Because it's not in the active file. Because Colleen…is something else now, a friend. And anyway…the buzz with you is different."

"The buzz with *me*."

"Yes."

"What…is the buzz with me."

"You have an urban—an urbane buzz."

"*I'm* urban and urbane?"

"Yes."

"You're not exactly a country hick."

"Maybe not, but if there's anything urbane about me it's acquired. I grew up in farm country. Whereas you…are redolent of the city."

"Redolent of the *city*. Hm." She seemed to ponder. "And what is the buzz with Colleen that's different."

"Oh, Colleen…Colleen is home cooking. She's a down-home girl. Rochelle, you and I have much more in common. I'm not going to tell you Colleen isn't intelligent. She is. But she's not a book person. I need—if I'm going to be with someone—I need to be with a book person."

"Hm."

She said, "So you think we have more in common?"

"Yes. For sure."

"Why, then…do I still feel that it would be a gamble?"

"You shouldn't see it as a gamble."

"But I kind of do."

"Well…my persuasive powers fail."

"What's that from?"

"Coleridge I think."

"Yeah…Coleridge. Something…something. My powers fail. My *spirits* fail. Oh…can't place it."

Just then the waitress walked up, taking in that their plates and bowls were mostly empty and they weren't focusing on them.

"Well. How we doing?"

18

He was miffed at himself now. Not, of course, because he'd walked her to her car on the dark side street. Not because, when they turned to face each other beside the car, he'd taken her hand and levered her into a long mutually-alcohol-fumed hug and kiss. It was what he'd said when they'd taken a pause: "Rochelle, I'd love it if you'd come over."

He'd said it sensing that she'd rebuff it; he'd known that, after the long talk in the restaurant, things were floating in ambiguity, not resolved. And indeed she'd said, "Hm, Ken, I have to think about that. I have to think about things."

But—on the other hand—what if he *hadn't* said it? Wouldn't that have meant leaving things *too* open? After all, a tipsy kiss beside a car after a third date meant precisely nothing. Not even to offer something beyond that—wouldn't that have signaled being ready to let it slip away altogether? His offer had been a way of saying—"I hope this won't all slip away"—hadn't it?

So why be peeved at himself?

He was lying on his bed, hands folded behind his head, in the bedroom of his rented apartment—the upper floor of the house owned and lived in by Mrs. Taviston, a widow in her seventies. He'd been renting it from her for three years and it worked out well. This upper floor was somewhat dilapidated and the cracked paint high up on some of the walls cried out for a new coat; but that wasn't something he cared about. He had quite a large space for a young guy renting on his own, and Mrs. Taviston was quiet and agreeable and didn't jack up the price every year.

Now, as the rush of thoughts subsided, he felt the pulsing of his temples and the dizziness, saw the ceiling floating upward. Well, no way to escape such effects after three gin and tonics. He also realized—or recalled—that there were things, objects, that were making claims on his attention. What were they? Well, a couple of them were on the desk just to his left. The other—the vodka bottle—was out in the kitchen. It was the sole bottle of booze he had in the place. It was for times like this, when he was already on a wave and stopping it was more problematic than letting it continue.

He came back into the room holding a glass with a jostling ice cubes and a quantity of vodka. He went to the desk, set the glass down on it, and looked at pages strewn on it.

One of them was actually a set of two pieces of typing paper that—along with a copy—he'd brought to his meeting today with his thesis adviser, Professor Michaelson. Onto these pieces of paper he'd pasted four photocopied passages from the fiction of Thomas Wolfe that, he thought, illustrated the gist of the thesis he was proposing to write. Professor Michaelson had sat there glancing over them, already impressed enough with what Ken was proposing that he didn't need to bear down on them.

Now he took these two pieces of paper; set the glass with the vodka on the night table, turned on the lamp there, lay back on the bed, and held the pages before him in the lamplight.

He read:

I would drain the bottle to its last drop, feel for a moment its fatal, brief, and spurious illusions of deliberation and control, and then rush out into the streets of night to curse and fight with people, with the city, with all life. Into the tremendous fugue of all-receiving night was packed a century of living, the death, despair and ruin of a hundred lives. Night would reel about me lividly the huge steps of its demented dance, and day would come incredibly like birth, like hope, like joy again, and I would be rescued out of madness to find myself upon the Bridge again, walking home across the Bridge, and with morning, bright, shining morning, blazing incredibly again upon the terrific frontal cliff and wall of the great city.

Having whispered the last lines of the passage, he lay there with his eyes closed, holding the pages to his chest.

He opened his eyes and read the next one:

For suddenly you remember how the tragic light of evening falls even on the huge and rusty jungle of the earth that is known as Brooklyn and on the faces of all the men with dead eyes and with flesh of tallow gray, and of how even in Brooklyn they lean upon the sills of evening in that sad hushed light. And you remember how you lay one evening on your couch in your cool cellar depth in Brooklyn, and listened to the sounds of evening and to the dying birdsong in your tree....

He moved his eyes dully to the next:

> That spring the picture of these great vans at night, immense, sombre, and yet alive with a powerful and silent expectancy, the small green glow of the drivers waiting for the word to start, had given me a sense of mystery and joy. I could not have said what emotion the scene evoked in me, but in it was something of the cruel loveliness of April, the immense space and loneliness of the land at night, the lilac dark, sown with its glittering panoply of stars, and the drivers moving in their great dark vans through sleeping towns, and out into the fragrant country-side again, and into first light, cities, April, and birdsong in the morning.

"God, I love this stuff," he muttered.

Lay there again with the pages on his chest.

Finally he lifted them up again and read the last of the passages:

> It was now early morning, about half-past three o'clock, with a sky full of blazing and delicate stars, an immense and lilac darkness, a night still cool, and full of chill, but with all the lonely and jubilant exultancy of spring in it. Far-off, half-heard, immensely mournful, wild with joy and sorrow, there was a ship lowing in the darkness, a great boat blowing at the harbor's mouth.
>
> The street looked dark, tranquil, almost deserted—as quiet as it could ever be, and at that brief hour when all its furious noise and movement of the day seemed stilled for a moment's breathing space,

and yet preparing for another day. The taxis drilled past emptily, sparely, and at intervals, like projectiles, the feet of people made a lean and picketing noise upon the pavements, the lights burned green and red and yellow with a small hard lonely radiance that somehow filled the heart with strong joy and victory, and belonged to the wild exultancy of the night, the ships, the springtime, and of April....

He set the pages—again—upon himself, this time with something decisive and final about it.

After a few minutes he levered himself up, looked reflectively at the glass on the night table, took it and drank some of the vodka.

Setting the glass down again, he stood up—creakily and with much effort—and went back to the desk, where he set the pages back down and looked at the other pages that lay there to their right.

The sky-blue stationery of Colleen's letter.

He took these pages, too, lay down in the same way, and held them before him in the same way.

Dear Kenny,

I hope this finds you well! We haven't been in touch for a couple of months. You'll have to fill me in on the latest! By my calculations, you should be progressing now toward writing your thesis. Have you found a way to pay the bills in Binghamton for the summer? Give me the lowdown!

Over here, Scottie is breaking new records every day with his walking and talking abilities. I believe

the number of words he knows is now in double figures! At work, among other things, I have the sense
that I'm finally—after, admittedly, feeling despair at
some points—making progress with Kimberly. I believe I'm getting her to the point where she can stop
letting what happened to her control her. I'll be very
thrilled when—and if—I pray—she gets there.

So much for the good or at least hopeful stuff.
Now for the not-so-good stuff. Looks as if the you-
know-who problem has actually taken a turn for the
worse lately. I would actually have to say an unprec-
edented turn for the worse. Surprised that it could
actually get that much worse? Read on—and I'm
sorry if it's depressing!

You know, of course, who Justin is—oldest of
my three almost-unknown Colorado half-siblings.
Well, it looks like Justin has decided to break out of
the cocoon that his (and my) wonderful father has
woven around him (and his sister and his brother).
Justin finished his BA in economics this year at Colorado U., got into the NYU grad school, and now
on June 3-4th he's coming to New York to get a better
look at NYU and look into living possibilities. And…
surprise surprise…he says he'd really like to meet me
there on the afternoon of the 4th so we can get to
know each other a little better at last (he wants to
meet Billy too, but that's a little more complicated
with him being overseas!).

Kenny, I don't have to elaborate to you on how
eager I'd be to do that, how I've wished these people
would take the slightest interest in me—and now
one of them is actually doing so. But there's a hitch.

Yes. Guess who doesn't like me going there by myself to "meet a man." Yes, a man who is my brother; to meet him in a restaurant in the afternoon.

And at this point Reg is…implacable. He says why can't Justin come here. I said it's already a big hike from Colorado to NYC, and anyway it does not make any difference. And so, as of now, any kind of meeting is sort of in suspension. I try to raise it with him and he remains stone-faced and doesn't want to talk about it.

Now you may well be thinking—does he control me? Can he stop me from going there? And the answers are no and no. But, Kenny, I don't want there to be some kind of blowup here, some kind of terrible situation for Scottie to be exposed to. I did not bring him into the world to experience strife.

Talking about it with people at work—people who are supposed to be colleagues, supposed to be good with such problems—they propose various ways I can discuss it with him that will bring him around. They don't know Reg! (They may have encountered him at parties and events, but it's not the same thing!)

So at this point, dear Kenny, I really don't know how this one will play out. Whether he'll relent (long odds), or whether—I'll just go and meet Justin without his so-called "approval" and risk a blowup. Or whether—difficult as it is even to write it—I'll just give in. Kenny, you know about my fear of things not working out, coming unglued, of kids experiencing pain when they're still way too young and should not be experiencing such things. I wish I did not even have to think in such terms.

Dear Kenny, now that I've plied you with all this stuff, do let me know what's happening with you when you have a chance! And unless my husband has now totally gone off the deep end, we should be meeting again soon, in the summer I think! I know that you're out there, dear friend, and it does help!
Love,
Colleen

He held these pages to his chest, too; lay there like that, eyes closed.

PART FIVE: NOVEMBER 1986

19

In me thou seeth the twilight of such day
As after sunset fadeth in the west,...

Those were the words that came into his mind, even
though sunset hadn't yet faded; there was still a ridge of ragged
red light in the west, as he stood in the courtyard of the library
waiting for his sister.

It was a small library on the outskirts of Amherst, Massachusetts. Lizzie had studied library science at Amherst College,
and now she was an assistant librarian here. She'd talked with
her boss and succeeded to line up a lecture for him. A lecture
to a small book club, mostly middle-aged and older women,
that met in a room at the library.

He'd come all the way from Colgate University in central
New York State. His dissertation on Wolfe having impressed
some people and been turned into a book that was published
by a university press, he was now assistant professor of English
at Colgate. The real reason he'd come to Amherst wasn't—as
Lizzie knew—the lecture, for which, in itself, he wouldn't have
come all the way from Hamilton.

It was still before five o'clock, but the dusk was advanced.
It was November, and the air at this hour already had a dark,

still finality to it. The book club met at seven; Lizzie was supposed to be on her way from her apartment in the town and they were supposed to go somewhere to eat.

He stood there in the dusk stillness.

He heard her footsteps before he saw her. She wore a dark jacket and her thick, frizzy hair looked just as dark in silhouette. They hugged.

"What a jerk I am," she said. "You come from the other end of the world, and I keep you waiting."

"Aa, it's OK. I was early."

"Hungry?"

"Yeah, for sure."

"There's a little place here. It's pretty nice. Or we can go someplace nicer if we drive a little."

"I'm sure what's here is fine."

It *was* nice—a homey, unassuming, clean little café.

They took a table by a window; there was nothing to be seen by now but lights of passing vehicles.

She said, "Were you able to park?"

"Yeah. In the library parking lot. There were empty spaces. I guess people going home already."

"How's Rochelle?"

"Fine."

"She know the real reason you're here?"

Lizzie's carrot-colored hair and forthright blue eyes were the same as always, but her face was more thick and solid now. She was still overweight, more than when she was a teenager.

"She knows. She knows I wouldn't come all the way out here to talk to the book club."

"She OK with it?"

He made a face. "Not really."

A waitress came to their table, and they made their orders.

"So how you doing, Lizzie?"

"Oh, same stuff. Get up in the morning, go to work, go home."

"Not thrilling."

"Nope."

"Anything on the personal front?"

She looked sardonically at him.

"That's what mom and dad always ask me. Don't tell me you're worried about me, too."

"Ha, ha. Not worried. It can add a little spice to life. For better or worse."

"Yeah, spice. Something that enhances or something that's maybe too tangy."

"It can definitely go either way."

"Well. Not really. Not lately. Not since the thing with Jeff ended."

"From all that I heard about it, seems like it's better that it ended."

"Oh definitely. No second thoughts... I don't know. I should probably get going again. Start looking around again."

"So," she said. "What are you lecturing on?"

"Oh, on...some Hemingway lake stories."

"*Lake* stories."

"Yup."

"Hemingway wrote about a lake?"

"When he was a kid his family stayed at a lake in Michigan in the summer. He wrote—in my opinion—some of his best stories about that."

"And what sorts of thing happened at this lake."

"Lots of things. Some of them really terrible. Also romances. Failed romances."

"*Failed* romances."

"Yup."

"At a lake."

"Yup."

"Sounds kind of familiar."

"Yes, it does. Guess there are some things you just can't get away from."

"And what…will you be telling the ladies about these lake stories."

"Well…good question. I tried to whip something up last night. Something about the lake being tranquility, innocence, but what happens near, or on, the lake—not tranquil or innocent at all. The lake as unattainable serenity, blah blah."

The waitress came with their food, his coffee, Lizzie's Coke. He hadn't eaten for hours and was quite happy to be handed a plate with a thick avocado sandwich, a high heap of French fries, and a pickle.

"So how," she said as they were eating, "is it going with you and Rochelle?"

"Well. Not too well."

"You're still trying?"

"We've gone for tests now."

"Yeah? They find anything?"

"No. Inconclusive results. They don't know which one of us is causing it. Or if it's something about the two of us, they don't know what it is."

"Hm."

"I don't know… I would definitely prefer to have a kid, but if it's not possible I can live with it. Rochelle's different. It's pretty crucial to her."

"So what would it mean if…"

"If it can't be done?"

"Yeah."

"I don't know. If things were otherwise OK between us, I think she could live with it too if there was really no choice. Neither of us would be into adoption in particular. But…this combined with other things…I don't know."

"And what are those other things."

She said, "I mean, I think I know but…you know."

"Yeah. Well. She resents that I'm a prof now and she's not. I don't think her job now is bad at all. You know, she's acquisitions editor for the university press."

"Right."

"Looking for people they might want to write for them, and writing to them to propose book ideas to them. Working with the authors to develop the books. Sifting through the stuff that people send in themselves and picking the stuff that seems promising. I don't see what's bad about that. She doesn't have all the damn tenure pressures that I have to deal with now."

"Hmmm. But…"

"But. She just sees what I'm doing as more glorious. That's just how it is."

"And she knows you're meeting Colleen tonight."

"Right."

"And she's not crazy about it."

"No."

He said, "Colleen and I aren't crossing any lines, if that's what you're wondering about. We haven't and we're not planning to."

"You met with Colleen in Springfield about a month ago, right?"

"Right."

"That's what I was wondering about. I thought that these meetings happened once every quite-a-few months. So...I was just curious as to why it seemed kind of urgent for you to meet with her now, kind of soon after the last meeting."

"Yeah. She's in a lot of distress."

He said, "She told Reg that I'm 'lecturing at Amherst.' Which is true—in the town of Amherst. He thinks it's at the college, or maybe the university. So, let him think it. I came up with this whole thing. We could have just dispensed with the lecture to the book club. But then she'd have had to tell Reg a lie-lie, a lie of commission. This way it's just a lie of omission—'He's lecturing at Amherst,' which is true."

"You're a sly one."

"Yes, I have to pat myself on the back for this one."

"Although...one would say 'in' Amherst, if it wasn't at the college."

"True. Well, 'at,' 'in.' It's not that much of a difference. Even my ruses aren't perfect."

She laughed.

"I kind of thought, though—I mean, from what I know about it—that Reg doesn't let her do things like that in any case. Driving somewhere at night to see you. Even if it's a lecture at Amherst."

"Yeah, Colleen changed the terms years ago. There was a big crisis where he was trying to stop her from meeting with her brother—her half-brother Justin—in New York. He was jealous even about that, meeting with her brother. So in that case Colleen just finally decided to defy him and she did it anyway. It didn't work wonders between her and Reg but it was good that she did it because since then she doesn't knuckle down to him as much. She and Justin are good friends now, by the way. The only one of her half-siblings who shows any interest in her."

"But, like...she doesn't visit you in Hamilton."

"No. No need to provoke Reg unnecessarily. I don't mind driving to Springfield now and then."

"And she—made tonight a special case. Since you're—lecturing at Amherst."

"Right. But...the idea was mine. She didn't say, 'I'm in distress, come out here and save me.' It's just...hard for me when it's like that. I needed to see her."

"Hmmm... So what's this distress that Colleen's in?"

"Oh, boy."

He unconsciously watched his finger making a digging motion at the table.

"Reg, he's...he's just getting worse and worse. You know that Colleen's got two kids now?"

"Yeah. She had a little girl. Few years ago, right?"

"Right. So...you might have thought that as the family consolidates like that, he'd calm down. But he doesn't. He's... he's verging on paranoia now."

"Paranoia."

"Yeah, it's...it's beyond making wild accusations at Colleen. He's convinced now that she's carrying on something with a guy at work. A fellow shrink, a colleague. There's no truth to it whatsoever. She doesn't even consider him an attractive guy...but Reg, he's convinced of it. So what he's doing, he's starting to retaliate, so-called. Carrying on something with a woman at the school where he works. He's a history teacher, you know."

"Right."

"Carrying something on, and telling Colleen about it—to get back at her, so to speak. Except Colleen's not sure if there's really something going on or if he's just making it up, or embroidering it. But it's none too pleasant."

"Definitely not. *He* needs a shrink."

"I know. Refuses. Hands down. Always has."

She exhaled with her cheeks puffed out.

"Can Colleen really put up with this?"

"Yeah. That's a good question. She's so, so committed to the family, so, so scared of breaking it up, because of what she went through after her family broke up when she was a kid."

Lizzie sat there thinking.

She said, "I don't know how mom and dad did it."

He said, "What?"

"Married thirty-five years. They get along. They love each other. They both really like their work. What's wrong with their lives?"

"Not much that I can see."

He said, "We don't seem to have the formula, do we."

"N-nope."

He said, "I'm not sure at all that Rochelle wants to keep going with me."

She moved her blue eyes to his.

"She says that?"

"She hints at it."

He said, "She was aware of the Colleen issue from the start. She says she convinced herself that I'd get over it. But lately…"

He raised his hands and dropped them on the table.

"Is she right?"

"What? That I'm hung up on Colleen? Yes."

She looked at him with a soft glow.

"You always have been."

"I know."

She said, "I could see it already back then when you first met her. At the lake. That afternoon when the two of you came back from the rowboat ride, and her parents started bawling her out. Oh God, you were upset."

He nodded his head, laughed. "Yup."

He said, "I was already her protector. Or so I thought."

She said, "I would think you both must be feeling pretty tempted. You know. Both of your marriages having trouble."

"What, that we free ourselves and hook up with each other?"

"Yup."

He sighed.

"It would mean becoming a stepfather to two kids."

"What's bad about that?"

"I don't know, Lizzie. I've never been a father. I'm supposed to become a stepfather? How do I know I could handle it?"

"I think you could."

"Really?"

"Yeah. You know how to be patient. You know how to listen to people."

"Well, thanks."

He said, "But I really don't think Colleen's going to divorce anyway."

"No?"

"Nope."

They sat silently. The waitress came by to ask if they wanted the dessert menus.

20

The lecture went better than he'd anticipated. He was aware that he was connecting emotionally with what he was saying, that it amounted to raw material for an article he could write up and send to journals. Particularly what he heard himself saying about Hemingway's story "The End of Something"— the total contrast between the placidity of the lake, the sunset, the moonrise, and the destructive turmoil within Nick. The question-and-answer session was quite lively; he could see that they'd keenly latched onto his words.

Lizzie, who'd introduced him as "my egghead brother," sat quietly to the side as he held forth. At the end she came up to thank them and tell them about the next lecture, and asked for an ovation for him, which they supplied with smiles.

When he went out with Lizzie to the lobby of the library, Colleen was already there. She gave a smile that took in Ken and landed on Lizzie; she said "*Lizzie!*" as they ran to each other, and they hugged like long-lost sisters.

"I haven't seen this girl," Colleen said to Ken, "in sixteen years."

"Is it sixteen?" Lizzie said.

"Yes. And you have *not* changed."

"Oh Colleen, I was going to say that about you, but please don't say it about me, come onon...."

"Really Lizzie. You haven't."

"Well. Then your memory's not good."

"My memory is *great*."

Colleen looked at him.

"And as for you, sir."

She came to him and they hugged—without kissing, but not trying to hide the depth of it from Lizzie.

They unlocked, and she stepped back, smoothed her hair back, looked at him.

Thirty-two now, Colleen had returned to letting her hair flow in long, thick, profuse waviness far down her back. Her face had careworn lines, rough skin at the corners of the mouth. Her eyes had the same amiability but with something glum in the depths.

"And how are you, professor," she said.

"Great."

"How was your lecture?"

"Nice. Better than I expected."

"He talked about a lake," Lizzie said.

"A *lake*," Colleen said, looking from Lizzie to him.

"Yeah," he said. "I guess there are some things you can't get away from."

She said, "Guess not."

"I know that you guys," Lizzie said, "have a lot to say to each other. Don't worry, I'll leave you to yourselves. But. If you want to go someplace in town, I can suggest some places to you."

Colleen looked from her to him.

"I'm not sure," she said. "I can't get back late."

He said, "We can just hang around here."

"Where are you going to sleep, though?"

"I'm driving back tonight. It's fine. I don't teach till the afternoon, I can sleep in the morning."

"*Kenny.*"

"It's fine."

They decided to just stay at the library grounds and find a place to sit. It was easy: in front of the building there was a flower garden, and along the garden there was a wall a few feet high.

They sat beside each other, against the wall, in the cool grass to the side of the garden. The library was closed now, and the place was dark and still. It was a clear, late-autumn night with keen, fiery stars.

They sat with his arm around her and her head on his right shoulder. They both wore thick jackets.

He said, "Alone together. Can't believe it. When was the last time? Sitting by the sea at your college?"

He said, "Then you wouldn't even let me get near you."

She said, "Little difficult when you're sitting upright in the sand with no backrest and you're in clear sight of the café up on the hill."

He said, "Right. That won't do. And since then it's always someplace really public like a café."

"Poor Kenny. What can I say."

He said, "'She cannot fade, though thou has not thy bliss....'"

"What's that?"

"It's from a poem by Keats. About a Greek urn. There's a fair youth and there's a maiden but they're stuck at what they're doing since they're figures on an urn and they can't move. But the maiden cannot fade, though he has not his bliss."

"Well, that sure sounds like it."

She said, "Oh God, Kenny."

She said, "That you came all the way here tonight. And you didn't tell me you're driving back the same night."

"I couldn't have stayed overnight at a motel or whatever. Rochelle wouldn't have believed anything I'd have told her. Even if I said I was staying at Lizzie's she wouldn't have believed it."

He said, "Second of all, I couldn't not come here. Couldn't not see you with all the crap that's going on. And on top of that it worked out well for me. Got to talk with Lizzie. And the lecture went better than I thought it would. I think I can turn some of what I said into an article."

"That's good."

"Yup."

"You talked about a lake?"

"When Hemingway was a kid his family would stay at a lake in Michigan in the summer. He wrote some stories based on it. I talked about how the quietude of the lake contrasts with the stuff, mostly a lot of bad stuff, that goes on in the stories."

"That rings a bell."

"Actually in a couple of the stories the lake is quite stormy, too. But I didn't tell them about that."

"No. Course not."

"I talked mostly about a story called 'The End of Something.' A guy and a girl are in a rowboat on the lake. In utter tranquility, at sunset, fishing. But the guy's got all kinds of dark turmoil inside, and he ends up breaking up with the girl."

She looked at him.

"You should be able to get something out of that."

"Yeah, I think so."

"But it should be the girl who has the dark turmoil."

"Well. Hemingway almost got it right."

She rested her head back against the wall.

She said, "Kenny…"

She said, "Your sister is so sweet."

"She's nice."

"I didn't think I'd be so emotional to see her. It's not like we were great buddies back then."

"I don't think you ever said anything to her but 'Nice to meet you.'"

"Ha, ha."

She said, "But I love her because she's you. Your sister."

She sat silently.

She said, "Kenny…if only I wasn't such a bitch that morning at the lake."

"The world conspired to make you a bitch."

He said, "And if you hadn't been one, maybe Scottie and Annie wouldn't have been born."

He said, "Or maybe there'd have been a couple of kids named Scottie and Annie, but they wouldn't have been the same ones."

He said, "Or maybe there wouldn't have been any kids, because you might have been with a man who can't have kids."

"Kenny. You don't know that."

"I don't know it. But it's possible."

He reached out, moved his hand around her head, and started stroking her hair.

"Don't do that Kenny."

She dropped her head down into her hands; he moved his hand away.

He said, "We try to help each other, and we just harm each other."

"Don't say that. It doesn't harm me that you came here. I'm glad that you came here."

He said, "Maybe that's all we're allowed to have. An island."

"If that's all we're allowed to have I'm glad we have it."

She raised her head from her hands again. He put his arm around her shoulders again; she again moved closer to him, though not putting her head on his shoulder.

He said, "So. Developments?"

"Yeah...yeah."

She said, "People at work are saying I should give Reg an ultimatum."

"An ultimatum."

"Yeah. That he goes for therapy or...I'm out."

"That makes sense."

"It does but...what if he won't do it. You don't know what fear that causes me."

"Because then you're supposed to...unravel it yourself?"

"Unravel it myself."

She pressed her fingers to her forehead.

"Fear for you or for Scottie and Annie?"

"For them."

"Is it good for them to be exposed to conflict?"

"No. They're not exposed to that much of it. But the atmosphere's bad...and they're picking up on it. Annie picks up on it more than Scottie does. Or maybe she just shows it more."

She said, "Kenny, if it breaks up it'll be bad. *He'll* be bad. He'll tell the kids that I'm a bad woman. My friend Helen's ex-husband does that. He trashes her to the kids, all the time."

"You really think he'd do that, though?"

"I wouldn't put it past him. Or he'll try to get custody. I wouldn't put that past him either."

"He wouldn't stand a chance."

He said, "Colleen, you can't allow yourself to be intimidated."

"I know, Kenny. I know… But it could be bad for them. It's not a question of what I think or what I feel. It's that it could be bad for them."

"Colleen. Sometimes your urge to do good gets the better of you."

"Yeah?"

"Yeah. If you're in a bad situation, you have to get out of it. And take it from there."

"I'm not ready to give up on it yet."

"What. You think the ultimatum might work?"

"It might. If I put it to him like that. He *cannot* take the thought of losing me. He can't."

"And you think therapy might do the trick for him?"

"Who knows. It might be worth trying."

She said, "It got me out of that jungle I was in."

"Yeah, but you were never a screwed-up person by nature. With Reg it's by nature."

"That may be true. Maybe it can help him. I don't know…."

He moved his arm—which was feeling strained—away from her shoulders; he moved it down and slipped his hand into hers.

They sat there quietly. The feel of her hand stirred reactions in him he would never have tried to describe. He told himself that if they had been together, together for years, the mere touch of her hand couldn't have caused such emotions in him. *She cannot fade….*

He said, "Is, uh…have you found out anything more about him and that woman?"

"Oh, that."

She sighed.

She said, "Kenny…if you get me talking about that…it'll make me want to kiss you."

"What. To get back at him?"

"Something like that."

"So do it."

"No."

"Why?"

"Because it won't stop."

"So what?"

She sighed.

He said, "I know. Conservative Catholic girl at heart."

She said, "A friend of mine at work knows someone who works at the school. She—this person at the school—says that Reg and the woman are together a lot. They hang out. You know, in the faculty lounge. They laugh and talk together all the time. If there's something going on beyond that, nobody knows about it for sure."

She moved her hand away from his, pressed both hands to her forehead.

"Such a creep. Because I never, never did anything like that. Even with you I didn't. They *all* know that he's married, and they *all* see him with her like that…."

He put his arm around her again. He pressed her to him close.

She said, "He really thinks I'm doing things with men. He really thinks that. He *really thinks* he has to get back at me."

He said, "There could only be a clinical cure for it. If at all."

She said, "OK. What's with Rochelle?"

He sighed.

"With Rochelle."

"So…they can't figure out what's causing it?"

"Nope."

She said, "Are you still trying?"

"Yeah, but...sporadically. It's like our hearts aren't really in it."

He said, "I think she wants to end it."

She sat very still. "Why?"

"Why?" He shrugged.

"I guess it's...having a kid means a lot to her. She probably thinks she might have a chance with someone else. And...we're not getting along that well. She thinks I rushed to take the job at Colgate and didn't think about where she was going. She's not happy with her job at the press. She feels that she sacrificed herself for me.... And...the other thing."

"Me?"

"Yeah."

She sat still.

"What does she say about that?"

He shrugged.

"I don't know. You know... 'There's another woman in my heart.' That's what she says."

She said, "This is not what I wanted."

"Colleen. It's not the main factor. If she was pregnant now, or if we had a kid, we'd be together. Things would be fine. More or less."

He said, "If I'm on the way out, maybe it's not the worst thing in the world."

"Why?"

"Because you might be on the way out too."

She said, after a time, "You always said you couldn't be a stepfather. That you couldn't handle it."

"I know. So, I'm older now. And...it might be the only way I could ever be some kind of father. So maybe I feel differently about it."

She said—again after a pause—"We've never been in a relationship together."

"I know."

He said, "One could even say there are ways in which we don't know each other."

She said, "Do you know that I still love Reg?"

"Yes."

She said, "Kenny. What does this night know that we don't know?"

"I don't know. What?"

"How to be at peace."

"Yes," he said. "This night is good at that."

"We can't stay here much longer."

"I know. I don't care what time I get back. You, obviously, can't get back late."

She said, "I wasn't designated for peace. There's probably a better word than designated, but you know what I mean."

"Yeah… Maybe you weren't."

"I seem to undergo something peaceful only when I'm with you."

"Well…maybe that's because we're on an island together that isn't real life, so things are simpler."

"I want to stop thinking."

She said, "I want to stop trying to figure things out."

"So let's stop."

They sat there, his arm around her, bodies pressed tightly together.

He thought: She's here. In my arm. Next to me. I feel her.

She said, after a time, "I want me, Reg, Scottie, and Annie to stay together. If at all possible. If at all bearable."

"I understand."

She said, "I don't like to hear that you and Rochelle may be splitting up. I think it's sad."

"I think it is too. I don't feel good about it."

"Is it because of me that she wants to leave you?"

"No. I told you. It's not something she likes. But it's not the reason."

He said, "I wish there was nothing but this."

"What. This?"

"Yeah."

"Be a lot simpler."

He said, "The stars, you know...the closest one—if you were traveling 186,000 miles a second—it would take you four years to reach it."

"That's pretty far."

"Some of those—I don't know which ones—are planets. They're a little closer. There are already spaceships floating around them taking pictures of them."

"I know. It's so cool."

He said, "'Yet some say Love by being thrall / And simply staying possesses all / In several beauty that Thought fares far / To find fused in another star.'"

"What's that?"

"It's from a poem by Robert Frost."

"Try it on me again?"

"'Yet some say Love by being thrall / And simply staying possesses all / In several beauty that Thought fares far / To find fused in another star.'"

"Need your commentary on that, prof."

"Well, it's basically saying that the things of most value are the things close to home. The things you've always had."

"The things you've always had, and have...and will have. In one way or another."

PART SIX: OCTOBER-NOVEMBER 1995

21

Once I was a kid in Willowcreek Park. A kid. Thinking life was essentially something that happened in the future, that everything happening so far was preparatory, and the future held limitless potential. In early spring, the snow gone and the evenings cool and blue, we'd gather again at the courts. Leon and I would meet there before others came. We'd shoot baskets and talk; the ball rattling the rim was like punctuation. About what would happen. About which girls we'd be with. About all the great things that were before us—in the future, where life was located.

Now the future—a sizable piece of it—had transpired. Leon was not only not part of it, he was long gone. Leon, broad and sturdy with his genial, confident grin, his ambling gait. His belief that he could do it all, could encompass everything—good and bad. Good grades, good athlete, good with the girls; at the same time cheerfully and lustily bad and wild, partying and drinking. Leon whose small, aged parents now came to visit him bearing flowers, gazing at the simple words and numbers carved on a stone.

And what of Professor Kenneth Wasserman? Still circulating, still observing winter-spring-summer-fall, but likewise untethered: a Wolfe-man wandering the earth without (?) an anchor, without a "home" to look back to except an apartment where he lived by himself.

Such thoughts kept coming to him now that, for the first time, he'd started living—for a relatively long span, the better part of a year—far from anything that could ever have been called home. After some years at Colgate, he'd been picked for the position at Dartmouth, and of course he'd taken it. After five or six years at Dartmouth, an email had turned up from the head of the Department of General Literature at the Hebrew University of Jerusalem—one Professor Ilan Cordova—saying that, if he had plans for a sabbatical, they would be happy to host him for a year. He would have an office and (but he didn't need one) a research assistant, and would just have to teach one course per semester, in American literature, at something called the Rothberg School for Overseas Students.

He thought of how he'd always wanted to get back to Israel sometime—and now it was inviting him. He thought how, in one way, the timing was perfect—if he really wanted to get serious about writing *Thomas Wolfe's "Of Time and the River" as American Anti-Epic*. He thought how, in another way, the timing was unpropitious—because it would mean being distant from Colleen just as she and Reg looked like they might finally be heading for the finish line. He thought about those things, and he communicated with Colleen, and he decided to answer Ilan Cordova positively.

The university said that, if he preferred, they could arrange for him an apartment to rent in something called French Hill, an adjacent neighborhood. Very relieved that someone was offering to do this for him—instead of having to do it himself, something he disliked and felt incompetent about—he told them, to go ahead.

It turned out French Hill was stunningly beautiful: buildings of golden stone under Mediterranean blue amid green pines, all within walking distance of the campus. His apartment was on the top, seventh floor of a building; its view grazed the rooftops of French Hill and landed majestically on Mount Scopus where the university was.

It was October, and the dazzling light on the golden stone, the gleaming azure of the sky, were like nothing he'd experienced back home. People strolled around him chattering in Hebrew; when he went to the supermarket, the bank, he spoke—sheepishly—in English. They could all manage it—usually with heavy accents, awkwardly, with mistakes; but he felt that *he* was the one who was remiss for being unable to manage in Hebrew. Twenty-four years ago on the kibbutz, when he was a kid, it had been easier to deal with; the Israeli kids had simultaneously made fun of his ignorance and taught him words, only few of which he still remembered. Now it was a bit of an ordeal, having to accost people in English; having to announce his foreignness, his ignorance. Again—like twenty-four years ago—he had the strange sense that he was *supposed* to be here, even though, by the age-old rules, he didn't count as a Jew.

There was, at this time, a peace process, but there were also bus bombings and other horrendous incidents. Not a few of the bus bombings and other incidents were in Jerusalem itself. So people back "home" said—you're doing this *now*? Why don't you at least wait a year or two, see if things calm down? He knew what the answer was but he didn't say it to them.

It was that—if he avoided going there for *that* reason—he would just have contempt for himself. Even though he wasn't considered an insider.

Some people said the peace process was proceeding successfully and the bombers were just retrograde religious fanatics. Others said the process was flawed and the bombers actually represented something deep-seated in the other population. He asked his intensely political, Jewish father what *he* thought. He said the latter view was right, and he gave what seemed like solid evidence for it. He said the process was flawed because the other side wasn't really ready for it yet, and things would keep being bad—dangerous—unless and until Israel woke up. When he told his father that, even though his words sounded persuasive, he was going there anyway, his father said, "I wish I could be there too."

He woke up in the morning in French Hill when the sun was already brilliant on the stones, limning the leaves of the bougainvillea in the courtyard below. It seemed to him almost unutterably beautiful that soon he would walk through the sunlight, the Hebrew, the flowers and stones, to his office at the campus. On one hand, he felt—in a way he couldn't admit to others, had trouble admitting even to himself—that *this* was a kind of "home." On the other, he felt that—and this was propitious—he now understood better than ever what it was to be Wolfe, a drifter on the planet with a trail of nostalgia and loss behind him.

Even though, today, he was supposed to meet Irina for lunch. How did that fit into the scheme? He didn't know. He didn't even know why he was doing it. Drifters just went from one thing to another....

But before he got going, there was this thing called email. He'd only had personal email for about a year, and it was a pretty remarkable thing. You could be in touch with people, you could just chat, transmit a piece of news or two, without having to engage in that old, often burdensome task known as "writing a letter." It was especially good, too, for a time like this when he was far from all of them back in the States.

This morning, as he sat down, holding a steaming cup of coffee, before the PC on the desk in his bedroom, there was an email from LizAnders—that is, Lizzie. It was a bit before 7 a.m. in Jerusalem, a bit before midnight in Tarrytown, New York, but the email had arrived only a short time ago. He knew that these days Lizzie often kept late hours—even though she had to get up early, get her son to the day care center, and get to work.

Lizzie had—almost incomprehensibly—married Duane Anderson. They had all—his father, his mother, him—tried delicately to urge her not to. Duane Anderson bounced from job to job—when Lizzie met him he was a waiter in a sushi restaurant—and loved hanging around bars at night. Even after he and Lizzie got started, he kept going to bars at night—supposedly—by himself. Lizzie remained quietly resolute; she implied that it was late in the game for her, she said Duane was fun to be with. After about a year they got married in Amherst. After about another year—because of some unexplained complication in Duane's life—they had to leave Amherst, and Lizzie found a job in a library in Tarrytown, up the Hudson from New York City.

Lizzie was divorced now, and Paulie was three years old. He was no picnic; demanded things fanatically, had fits and threw toys if he didn't get them right away. Lizzie had put on more weight, and she smoked cigarettes—a habit she'd picked up from Duane. Duane was now out West somewhere, and there hadn't been any child-support payments in months.

The email said: "Kenny, still alive? Please advise."

He replied: "Vital stats reading—positive."

It took only a couple of minutes for an answer to arrive: "Don't you want to keep it that way?"

KWasser: Affirmative.

LizAnders: Then why don't you get out of that place?

KWasser: Your daily revelation…EVERYBODY HERE ISN'T DYING.

LizAnders: Kenny why are you doing this to me? Don't you think my life's enough of a pain in the ass already? I know, I brought it on myself, blah blah…

KWasser: You think everybody's dying here because if you see anything on TV from here, it's only when there are people dying. Well, you might not believe it but mostly people don't die here, they live.

LizAnders: Kenny come on. Buses blowing up is not a normal situation. I'm not saying Tarrytown is paradise. But no buses blowing up.

KWasser: I don't take buses. If I have to get anywhere in town I take a taxi.

LizAnders: So why does anybody take buses.

KWasser: A lot of people can't afford fifty shekels each way to get to work and back on a taxi every day.

LizAnders: Sounds like a wonderful way to live.

KWasser: It's great here, Lizzie.

LizAnders: Yeah?

KWasser: Yup.

LizAnders: What's great?

KWasser: You wouldn't believe how beautiful this neighborhood is. It's not like anything at home. It's a different climate.

The people are calm and pleasant. At least here they are. I can't speak for other places in Israel. But here you wouldn't believe how pleasant it is to walk around and do stuff, even if you have to be a foreigner forcing people to speak English.

LizAnders: Are you teaching that course yet?

KWasser: Yes. It's nice. The kids seem nice and like they want to learn. Maybe it's because they know how much it's costing their parents to send them here for a year.

LizAnders: That's all you have to do?

KWasser: Pretty much. And I work on the book I'm writing, though nobody's looking over my shoulder to see if I'm working on it. They set me up with an office and a computer, and the library's nearby though I don't need it because I've already pretty much amassed the stuff I need and I brought it with me. Actually I don't need the office to work on the book—it's nicer and simpler right here in the apartment. But that wouldn't be nice, not using the office they gave me.

LizAnders: No, that wouldn't be nice, a touch ungrateful. What's with Colleen?

KWasser: Oh, boy... So far I haven't heard from her. You know that she's separated now from Reg? She's worried that he might have some detective tailing her. It's not a paranoid fear because he's capable of it. So she's very scared to contact me in any way, email or phone, because she thinks it could get picked up. She doesn't have a computer at home anyway, she uses the one she has at work, which is even more problematic.

LizAnders: Yikes...you're just out of touch?

KWasser: Her best friend Wendy has my email, so she could get in touch with me if, God forbid, there was something I needed to know about.

LizAnders: Didn't Reg get better for a while?

KWasser: He seemed to. You remember that night years ago when you got me the lecture at the library in Amherst, and Colleen showed up there?

LizAnders: Of course.

KWasser: Well very soon after that—I'm pretty sure I told you about this—Colleen gave him an ultimatum. That he'd get therapy for his problem or she'd divorce him. It did seem to work because he did go for therapy, for a few years, and did seem to get better. They even had the third kid, Timna. But after a while the effect wore off, I guess. He went back to accusing Colleen of all kinds of crazy things, crazier than ever. They had bad fights in front of the kids—at least in the past they didn't do that, in front of the kids. So a few months ago she told him it was finished. He didn't agree at first, but after a while he moved out. But he's going for custody now. He's nuts. Turns out he kept a log of every time Colleen and I met during the years they were married. He and his lawyer think they can prove there's something between me and Colleen, but it's a crock because we never did anything. Even if we did they couldn't prove it.

LizAnders: Oh my God. Kenny. He wants custody over three kids?

KWasser: So he claims. I think it's just a way to get back at Colleen.

LizAnders: How on earth is Colleen holding up under all this?

KWasser: Not easily. Scottie's a problem now too. He's seventeen now and he's running around with a bad crowd and making all sorts of problems. I didn't want to come out here now with all this going on, but Colleen really insisted. I'd been planning on it already for almost a year. I talked about putting it off, but she wouldn't hear of it. She said the timing was too good for working on my book. She said she refused to be an obstacle. She also knew I had kind of a yearning to get back to Israel sometime.

LizAnders: Wasn't she scared about you being over there?

KWasser: She was, but she knew how I felt about that—that I couldn't let it stop me.

LizAnders: Guess she's got a lot of understanding.

KWasser: She does for sure.

LizAnders: Wish I could get a hold of some of it.

KWasser: Lizzie, how you doing?

LizAnders: Kenny, what can I say. I have hopes for the future. That Paulie will be more independent, he'll be able to occupy himself more, and I'll have more time for myself again, and not in the middle of the night. It would help if I lived closer to mom and dad, but I don't, and that's that. Anybody who thinks I've got the strength to do another job search is on drugs.

KWasser: Is the job OK though?

LizAnders: Yeah Kenny it's OK. I get a kick out of being a librarian, I have no idea why. So there's that at least. It's when I get home that it gets rough.

KWasser: It should ease up eventually, like you say. I've got the easy part with Paulie. Just being an uncle. I miss him.

LizAnders: Have they got something like Christmas vacation there?

KWasser: Yes, for the universities at least. It's called winter vacation. I'll definitely be coming for a visit, so I'll bring y'all gifts and stories from the Holy Land.

LizAnders: That'll be cool.

KWasser: I should run along now, my office is longing for me.

LizAnders: OK. Kenny. Let me know if there's any kind of development with Colleen, OK?

KWasser: Sure.

LizAnders: And don't ride a bus or I'll kill you.

KWasser: You won't have to.

LizAnders: Ha ha.

KWasser: On that note…

LizAnders: Bye.

KWasser: Bye. Get some sleep, if you see that as a possibility at all.

LizAnders: I'll think about it. Bye.

Taking his coffee to the living room window, he stood there and looked at the morning sunlight. It filled the sky with a radiance that seemed beyond anything in the climate he was used to. "…to find myself upon the Bridge again, walking home across the Bridge, and with morning, bright, shining morning, blazing incredibly…"

22

The moment he'd seen Irina, he'd sensed that she would be an issue. By now his intuitions about such things were strong—all too strong.

The department was small, with only five or six members—all of them immigrants to Israel from various countries—occupying the offices along the narrow hall. Dr. Irina Pedayev—senior lecturer in Russian literature—had the office directly across from his. He'd first seen her at a moment when they both opened their doors simultaneously. It was the way she looked, and the way she looked at him. It wasn't the look of a woman who was married or attached to someone—or if she was, the man was someone to feel sorry for.

So far he hadn't talked with her much. She was very eager to talk with him; he was less eager about it. He was pleasant with her but subtly maintained—or tried to—a distance. So far he'd found out that: Her family had immigrated from Moscow when she was fifteen. By now she knew Russian, Ukrainian, Hebrew, English, and some French. She taught courses in Russian literature, and the students were mainly other Russian immigrants. She was divorced and had two small kids; he would have guessed her age at thirty-two or thirty-three. Her looks left nothing to complain about.

And now—why not admit it—the inevitable had happened; he had a lunch date with her that day. It was at the Maiersdorf cafeteria—a spacious, agreeable place with (to him at least) extraordinary falafel. He'd been there once before, but—never endowed with a keen sense of direction—was no longer sure how to find it. They were supposed to meet there at noon; she was busy elsewhere on the campus that morning. She'd suggested it to him during a chat in his office—"We should meet for lunch"—with a characteristic big, bright stare of her green, gold-flecked eyes. It was a stare that conveyed both enthusiasm for the person she was looking at and a certain sardonic coerciveness; it said, "You're not really going to turn down such a reasonable proposal, right?" And, of course, there was no way to turn it down, no way to cite reasons to do so even if they existed.

The campus was an interesting architectural scramble of old stone buildings going back to when the university was first built in the 1920s, and much more newfangled, geometrically complex buildings. It was aloft, almost three thousand feet high, and all of its winding, undulating paths led to stunning views—to the west, the dense, tawny buildings of the Arab part of Jerusalem towered over by the Dome of the Rock; to the south, the mythic, formidable, gut-tightening reaches of the Judean Desert; or, eastward, the purple Mountains of Moab rising like a phantom, like a biblical time warp. The foreground—winding paths, book-carrying students, flowerbeds—was calm, calmer than the American campuses he'd known. Most of the students were post-army—older, more grown-up, not here to have fun so much as to get started in life.

When he got to the cafeteria—having, in the end, given up on himself and asked for directions—Irina had been sitting in a little lobby just outside of it. When she saw him she rose up with a smile; she wore a white peasant blouse with a floral-print skirt. Her thick, glossy blond hair was back behind her ear on the right, down over her breast on the left. A pale, angular, northern-Ashkenazi face, with beauty in the earnestly intense eyes and in the pale delicacy of the mouth.

"Hi!" she said.

"Hi."

"Did you find it?"

"Sort of. I just blundered around…finally I asked someone."

She smiled. "I didn't think you would find it."

"No?"

"No."

"Well. Here I am. Somehow."

He ordered his falafel and Coke and she something much more elaborate, with fish, cabbage, potatoes, and salad. They carried their trays to a table at the rear of the cafeteria, by the picture window. He sat facing the cafeteria; she faced the view, a grassy slope leading to one of the lookout points over the Arab sector of the city. It was still on the early side and the place wasn't too full; there were students at some tables, a professor or two at others, as well as undefined, mostly foreign people, usually on some sort of academic business or just visiting.

She chewed some food and looked at him contemplatively.

"How is Wolfe?"

"Oh, fine."

He said, "Actually, Wolfe is never fine…. He's just leaving home and heading off for college."

"Why is that not fine?"

"For Wolfe things are sad. You don't just leave home. You pour out tons of nostalgia."

She sat glowing at him—an appreciative look, as if he were a lucky, unlikely find.

"And how is it for you? In your new college."

"Oh, I like it…. I'm elated to be here."

"Your first time in Israel?"

"My second time. I was here twenty…twenty-*four* years ago, I think. On a kibbutz. For two weeks."

"They made you do the work they were too lazy to do?"

"Ha, ha. You could say that. Some of the kibbutz kids did the work too, though."

He said—not sure why he was saying it, unless maybe a feeling that it needed to be gotten out of the way—"I'm not actually Jewish. Only my father's Jewish."

She gave him a slow, level look, softly contemplative.

"Only your father."

"Yes."

"With us—the Russians—that is not such a scandal."

"Yes. I know."

She said, "And what does this Jewish father do?"

"He's a writer."

"A *writer*."

"Yes."

"An American Jewish writer."

"Yes."

"Like Saul Bellow?"

"Well, I'm not sure about that."

"And how is he called?"

"Nathan Wasserman."

"Nathan… *Was*serman."

She said, "Why haven't I heard of him?"

"Because nobody has. He has just a small following. He's had the same publisher for—I guess—more than thirty years. They publish his novels, and I guess they—and he—make small profits from them."

She smiled.

"He must be very in-love with what he does."

"He is. There's nothing he loves more than writing novels."

"And how does your mother keep herself busy while he's writing these novels?"

"My mother is principal of a private girls' school. Also for a long time, also happy with it."

She gave him a bright, taken-aback look.

"They sound like lucky people!"

"They are."

"It sounds like they get through life smoothly."

"Yes. They do."

She held him in her still gaze.

"You were saying—I think—that you didn't always get through it so smoothly."

"No."

He looked guiltily down at his tray; delicately tamped a wayward edge of falafel back into the pita.

"I've, uh…"

He slowly raised his gaze back up to hers.

"I was married six years. Been divorced…I think it's seven years."

"Seven years."

"Yes."

"So. You have lost track of your ex-wife?"

"Lost track? No. We're in touch. Just a little. Couple of times a year, maybe."

"And what is she up to?"

"She lives in New York City now. She's an editor at Knopf. She's remarried. Has a couple of kids."

She looked at him brightly, intently.

"Not your kids."

"No."

"You didn't have kids with her."

"No… It was a fertility problem. So I guess…" He raised his hands and dropped them on the table. "The problem was with me."

Now her look was perturbed.

"But you don't know that. How do you know that?"

"I guess I don't, really."

"Sometimes it is something between the two people. Something specific to the two people."

"Yes. I know. It could have been that."

He said, "But. I'm not sure it makes much difference now."

She said, "Seven years. Divorced."

"Right."

She said, "Is it OK if I say something?"

"What?"

"I don't see how you could have lasted seven years. I think you're someone somebody would have snatched up by now. If you don't mind my saying it."

"Oh. Ha, ha."

He said, "I don't know, I…I haven't had much energy for it."

"Energy."

"Yeah…"

"No. You need your energy to write about Wolfe, and Fitzgerald!"

"That's part of it."

She kept looking at him—intently, from somewhere deeper than the conversation.

"And it's because you're sad. Like Wolfe. Like all the American writers. Fitzgerald, too."

"Yes, there's something to that. Not that I'm one of the writers."

She'd come to a stop; setting her fork and knife down, as if her food, however interesting, could no longer compete with him as a subject.

She said, "I feel like I have to push you along a little. To be with me. To be with me in the conversation. Do you know what I mean?"

"Oh…you shouldn't see it that way."

He said, "There's another woman in my life."

"Oh?" She said it with beautiful subtlety, her eyebrows arching.

"It's someone I met when we were kids. She's married now. But divorcing, it looks like."

"Di*vor*cing."

"Yes. It seems that way."

She said, "And you came out here? With this happening?"

"She insisted on it. She said the timing was too good—because it would give me time for my book. She said she refused to stand in my way."

"So. Are there plans for when you get back?"

"Plans? No… I really don't know what will happen. She has three kids…. I don't know if I could handle that. I've never been a father. All of a sudden…three kids."

"Would you have to move in with her?"

"Maybe not. One of the kids is small. A girl who's four years old now. Maybe I would have to."

"So," she said. "You are afraid of a woman with kids."

He raised his eyes to hers; he'd been staring downward and to the side.

"And of a woman who lives in a different continent."

She smiled. "You'll be in this continent for a while."

"Yes. But only a while."

"Or maybe I'm just not the right one for you."

"No. I wouldn't say that."

They both fell silent. The cafeteria was more crowded now; people were in the midst of their day, carrying trays, sitting down, leaning toward each other, laughing.

She said, "I am the kind who plays it by ear. It's true, I was impulsive before. It got me in trouble. What can I say? Maybe I just…can't learn."

"Learn…who can learn."

He said, "Life can only be understood backwards, but it has to be lived forwards. Kierkegaard said that."

"Kierkegaard?"

"Yes."

She smiled. "For that—just for saying that—he deserves to be famous."

"Yes."

He said, "It would be hard for me to jump into anything new. Not only because she's divorcing. I've been…hesitant like that. Since I got divorced."

She gave him a delicate, pensive look.

"Nobody has to jump."

"No."

She said, "I could sit here and talk all day, but I have to teach soon."

She said, "So. I scare you."

"Oh no, I wouldn't say that."

She said, "There are lovely restaurants in Jerusalem. But… we don't have to go to them."

He stared silently at her.

She said, "We could keep meeting here."

"Yes… That would be nice."

"If you want to. Whatever you want."

"Yes, that would be nice."

He said, "Do you have time next week?"

"Yes."

"Sunday?"

She shrugged. "Sunday is fine."

"Good. So let's meet on Sunday."

She said, "I will be teaching Turgenev in a few minutes. I didn't prepare for it. I will have to improvise."

"Oh. Well, that's a familiar experience."

23

That was on a Tuesday—the last day of October. When he got up the next morning he saw that—as if on schedule—the weather in French Hill had changed. The sky was grey with fog, the buildings dark with rain, losing their gold to a russet hue.

He felt his mood change, too, as days of rain continued. The early, simple elation over sunlight and flowers gave way to something more muted and complex. Images of Irina came to him; a sense of expectation over Sunday's meeting. What would it be like? What would happen? He knew what *would* happen— unless he stopped drifting passively like a branch on a stream. What was it that *he* wanted? But when he tried to look inside himself, no answer crystallized; instead it seemed lost in fog.

When Saturday—Shabbat—came, his mood got glummer. Still raining—though not continuously; he was learning that in Israel, even on rainy days, rain actually alternated crazily with sunlight gleaming through mists. He saw, down below, people making the most of these sunlit interludes to take their kids to the little playground that was beside a nursery school. He saw, too, that it wasn't an easy country to be alone in.

His parents had called last night, Lizzie had emailed with him; but now he found himself—as far as human contacts were concerned—lacking. The people in the department were nice, but there were few of them, and no friendships had formed apart from whatever was forming or not forming with Irina. It seemed he should take advantage of all this free, abundant time to work on his book; but he didn't. Something in him was too distracted, maybe too unsettled about tomorrow's lunch date; or maybe he was affected by the fact that this was supposed to be the Jewish day of rest. Instead—not even opening the computer file in which his book was being composed—he tried taking a walk; he saw French Hill with sodden grass and pearls of rain on the pines. But when—this was around two in the afternoon—he heard, for the first time in these days, a nervous mutter of thunder, he thought best to head back.

Back in his apartment, sitting at his living room window, feet up on the sill, he saw the sky grow dark and sullen as rain poured down more grimly and thunder rocketed about. He went to his kitchen, poured himself a glass of cabernet sauvignon, came back to the chair. After a while he saw—even now—sun breaking through again, rays glittering among swirling mists; but it didn't last long, soon the rain took over again. Now wicked forks of lightning turned the sky lurid and the thunder bellowed. He sipped the wine and—unhappily, since it was a tendency he'd been trying to fight—knew he'd keep sipping it.

After heating up a supper he took what he thought would be a nap on his bed; but the wine made it last longer, and when he finally woke up he had the bewildered sense that much more time had passed than he'd intended.

It turned out it was a quarter to ten. Apart from the lamp on the night table he'd turned on, the apartment was dark. From outside the rain sounded steady and resolute now. He turned on the TV. He couldn't believe what he saw.

He stared mutely for a few minutes. He fumblingly found the remote control, switched from the Israeli Hebrew channel to CNN. They, too, were already reporting it now, in English: Prime Minister Yitzhak Rabin, after a rally in Tel Aviv, had been assassinated in a parking lot. The assassin, who had been seized immediately by Rabin's bodyguards, was being called a "settler"; later it turned out he was a far-right student from the coastal town of Herzliya.

He sat watching in dull disbelief.

He heard, now, rumbles of thunder, low and sullen.

The TV was opposite the headboard of the bed; to the right, on his desk up against the window, was his computer.

He went, sat at the desk, and turned on the computer.

He went first into his Speedmail. Emails from his parents, from Lizzie, and from his colleague and best friend at Dartmouth, Nelson, had already arrived; there was also one from a username he didn't recognize: **wend-ur-way**.

He sunk his forehead in his hand. He felt a desire, but he had to wait awhile to get in touch with it, see what it was: to go to the kitchen and get some more wine.

Standing in the lighted kitchen pouring the wine into the glass, he thought: **wend-ur-way**. Wendy.

Turning out the light in the kitchen—responding to an unaccountable wish that it be dark there, too—he made his way slowly and carefully, knowing the wine was jostling, back to his dimly lit bedroom.

He gazed at the TV. He put it back on the Israeli channel, and saw the foreign minister, Shimon Peres, being interviewed.

He turned off the sound so that he could concentrate better on whatever the emails were saying to him.

He settled slowly, heavily back into the desk chair, sipped the wine, set the glass down beside him.

He opened **wend-ur-way**.

When he clicked on the username, the name Wendy Ursula Waylon appeared beneath it.

He gazed at the email itself:

wend-ur-way: Kenny it's me Colleen. I heard the news about the prime minister. I came over to Wendy's so I could get in touch with you. I had to bring Timna but she's fine, she's playing with Shirley. I am just stunned, I am just in disbelief. Is everything OK? I realize it's night for you but please answer if you get this!

Love,

Colleen

KWasser: Everything OK Colleen. At least I'm hearing from you!

wend-ur-way: Kenny it has been so hard being out of touch like this. What's going to happen? Is there going to be a civil war? Please keep yourself safe!!!!

KWasser: No civil war Colleen. There's a lot of anger between the right and the left but almost no violence. One person did this, an extremist. The whole country will be in shock.

wend-ur-way: Kenny if that's true I'm very relieved. Confession time: I've been worried sick about you being over there. I know I told you go go go, do not put it off because of me, and I still think I was right to say that. But I find myself—in the morning before I look at the newspaper—actually praying—*praying*—and you know I'm not so religious—that there hasn't been another terrorist attack. Kenny how are you? Has it been OK so far?

KWasser: Colleen it's been very nice. This neighborhood is unbelievably beautiful. For a couple of weeks there were just peaceful, sunlit, beautiful days. Now it's been raining but after all it's November. I'm getting work done on the book, and the class I teach is nice, it's English-speaking kids from overseas who mostly want to learn. So I'm doing fine.

wend-ur-way: Kenny that's wonderful. It sounds wonderful. It's been so hard to be out of touch and it's wonderful now to be in touch again even though it took such a terrible event to get it to happen. I have thought of emailing you from here but I ended up backing away from it because of my fears, or some might say paranoia. This email thing is unbelievable. This is the first time I've contacted someone outside the U.S., let alone on the other side of the world, and it's like you're right here.

KWasser: Yes, Colleen, it is amazing. But now you have to tell me how *you're* doing. I know that people are worried about me but *you're* the one who's in the tough situation, not me. How's it going? Has he calmed down at all?

wend-ur-way: Oh Kenny. Calmed down. I wish I could say so. The opposite. What he's done now is something you won't believe. If you remember that night we met years ago in Amherst—I'm sure you do—he got this guy who works for him, this detective, to look into whether or not you ever gave a guest lecture at Amherst College *or* U. Mass. at Amherst and of course the guy found out that you never did. So he thinks he's going to use this against me now—to say that I misled him that night so that you and I could be together. Which is of course true, but not in the way that in his paranoia he now thinks.

KWasser: Can't believe it. He's going off the deep end.

wend-ur-way: He is. For sure. My lawyer says it's nonsense, that he can't prove that anything happened that night and anyway something like that happening nine years ago won't have an effect on a custody question. And anyway I didn't tell him anything that wasn't true, I said you were lecturing in Amherst, which was true, I just didn't say where.

KWasser: Colleen this must be really tough.

wend-ur-way: I'm not going to say it's easy. Someone I knew for so long. Someone I thought I loved. And he just has this sickness in him and it just eats away at him and now it's taken over completely. Of course it's connected to other things about him that maybe I deceived myself about.

KWasser: How are the kids?

wend-ur-way: Kenny they're better than you might think. Scottie has his problems, I try not to think about it too much, these kids he's going around with, but next year he'll be at Framingham and I just hope it'll be better for him there and he'll settle down. Annie is fine, she's so sweet and supportive it's just unbelievable. In a way it's hardest with Timna because there's no way she can grasp what's going on. "Daddy went to live in another house because he and mommy weren't getting along," and she's made up her mind that it's something temporary and she's counting the days till he comes back. Kenny... why do the innocent have to get hurt.

KWasser: I wish I knew.

wend-ur-way: Kenny here I am rambling on and you're living in a country where there's been a disaster. Is it going to be OK there? Really?

KWasser: Yes Colleen it will. It's never been easy here. True, this is something new. But the society will pull together, it always does. *Ein breira*. That means "no choice" in Hebrew. When there's no choice you pull through.

wend-ur-way: Must be really strong people over there. And Kenny, how are you doing? Are you acclimating? You told me about your book and the class that you're teaching and that's great. And how is it for you? Are you making friends?

KWasser: I guess you could say making acquaintances. The department's very small, five or six people, immigrants from all over the place who teach foreign literatures. They've been nice and welcoming but I can't say any great friendships have come out of it. But it's fine.

wend-ur-way: Any women among these acquaintances? I bet there's something by now. There always is.

KWasser: Oh, that.

wend-ur-way: Yeah, that. Wendy is being so nice, she's giving the girls something to eat now to keep them occupied. She knows how much I've wanted to be in touch with you. So here I am pestering you.

KWasser: Not pestering, Colleen. Yeah, I suppose you could say there's something, but it's not much. There's someone I met for lunch last week and I'm supposed to meet her for lunch again tomorrow. But that's really all.

wend-ur-way: Yeah?

KWasser: Yeah.

wend-ur-way: Attractive?

KWasser: Yes, you could say attractive. Colleen.

He sent the email like that—unfinished.

He got up, clumsily, from the chair.

He went to the window; he slid the pane upward.

He saw that now—in the night—something had happened that was like what happened during the day. The rain had paused, or maybe there was still a fine drizzle; the air was raw and cold, the buildings deep-black against the dark sky;

high above, though, the moon had made its way through the dense fog and found a patch of space from which it was beaming brightly.

He gazed at it; he slid the pane shut again.

He glanced down at the wineglass beside the computer; it was almost empty. He'd been drinking from it as he typed, but he hadn't realized how much; it had been more than half-full when he brought it over.

He sat back—slumped was more like it—into the chair.

He peered at the screen. There was already a new email in it.

wend-ur-way: Kenny?

KWasser: Yes.

wend-ur-way: You just sent an email, but it didn't seem complete.

KWasser: It wasn't.

wend-ur-way: Oh. OK.

wend-ur-way: Why not?

KWasser: Because there's something I want to say.

wend-ur-way: Yeah?

KWasser: Yeah.

wend-ur-way: What?

KWasser: Well.

He left this email unfinished, without sending it; he drank what was left of the wine.

He sat back; he blinked while dizzy lights swam away from him.

He went back to the email; deleted the word, typed something else.

KWasser: There be none of beauty's daughters.

wend-ur-way: What?

KWasser: There be none of beauty's daughters.

wend-ur-way: What's that?

KWasser: It's from a poem by Byron.

wend-ur-way: Oh. Figures. I figured it was something like that.

KWasser: It starts like this:
There be none of beauty's daughters
With a magic like thee;
And like music on the waters
Is thy sweet voice to me.

wend-ur-way: It's pretty.

KWasser: Yes, it is.

wend-ur-way: What does it mean?

KWasser: Well, I don't know. It reminds me of something that happened to me once. A long time ago. On the waters.

wend-ur-way: What waters were these?

KWasser: Very peaceful, beautiful waters with sun sparkling on them. Then there was some kind of storm and it all got blown away.

wend-ur-way: That sounds like something that happened to me once, too.

KWasser: Oh, really?

wend-ur-way: Yeah.

KWasser: I think those waters are still there. Just as serene. Maybe not now, maybe not in November. But in the summer, I think they're still the same.

wend-ur-way: I think so too.

KWasser: I think we could be there again. We could go there again. In the summer. But without a storm.

wend-ur-way: I think we could too.

KWasser: Because it's all still there. It's all still the same up there. It doesn't change.

wend-ur-way: Never.

About the Author

David was born to Austrian Jewish immigrants in New York City in 1954. When he was four his family moved north to upstate New York, near the town of Schenectady, and David grew up there in an area where there was still farmland with pastoral vistas. Among his favorite activities were writing stories, mostly Westerns; playing a beloved game, basketball; and listening to music, ranging from classical to rock. But it took him until age seventeen to start becoming a pretty good self-taught pianist.

In 1978 David received an MA in English from Binghamton University. After that, already with a small family to support, he worked in Connecticut and then back in upstate New York as an English instructor, freelance writer, and freelance editor, while starting to build up a corpus of short stories. In 1984 he and his family made the big move to Israel—specifically, Jerusalem.

There David worked as English-publications editor at a research institute, but with many of the manuscripts arriving in Hebrew, and with his Hebrew improving, he began to try his hand at translating. Meanwhile—still in pre-Internet days—he was often publishing articles and book reviews in Israeli and American Jewish newspapers and magazines, and still finding time to write short stories that he began publishing in literary journals. And somehow amid all that he kept making progress on the piano, too.

Today David lives in the southern town of Beersheva, and his three grown kids live a little to the north and west in Tel Aviv and Ramat Gan. David is now a freelancer running a three-ring circus of writing, translating, and editing, and has by now published hundreds of articles, mostly about Israel, on popular Israeli and American sites. In recent years, though, he's put the emphasis back on his first love—writing fiction. That involves drawing on his various experiences and memories from America and Israel while, of course, adding a touch of imagination.

David's book *Choosing Life in Israel*, a selection of his articles, was published in 2013; his novel *You Don't Know What Love Is* in 2018; his collection *Help Me, Rhonda and Other Stories* in 2019; and, also in 2019, with Adelaide Books, his novel *Beside the Still Waters*.